FANGS FOR THE MEMORIES

FANGS FOR THE MEMORIES

PROVIDENCE PARANORMAL COLLEGE BOOK TWO

D.R. PERRY

CHAPTER ONE

Henry

The bronze circle looked burnished in the dim mezzanine light of the Nocturnal Lounge. I'd been exhausted when I finished it, and I couldn't remember that happening to me before. I wondered whether it had. I might have wiped the memory, storing a copy in some object not too different from this one. Memory was my business; copying, recording, sometimes deleting.

I could wash my hands of this project after sunset when I bound the amulet to the magus I'd made it for. She had Umbral Affinity, a rare talent that went with her magical energy. I'd had a friend with that talent up until 1989 just before the Big Reveal happened and the whole world found out about Extrahumans. She ended up dead in the same incident that made me a vampire.

"Hey, Henry!" I glanced into the lower level at a wiry dark-haired guy in a trench-coat. I wrinkled my nose, getting it used to the gamy scent of a shifter. With the amulet in my pocket, I headed down, trying not to look as reluctant as I felt. Being an introverted vampire with psychic powers wasn't usually a problem. Being one who had to go back to school after over so many years was a whole different ball of wax.

"Tony." I grinned at the cat shifter with my lips closed. He'd never seemed disturbed seeing vampire fangs before, but I didn't like showing them off.

"Lynn sent me. I'm here to bring you to your client." Once Tony Gitano stopped talking with his hands, like a good Italian boy, he poured a cup of coffee.

"Oh. Okay." I watched him dump five packets of sugar in his cup. Sometimes he took it with just milk and other times black. Nothing I knew about Tony made sense. That was par for the course with most feline shifters. I never knew back then exactly what type he was or how much he'd been through.

"You want some?" He stirred the cup briskly, then tossed the stirrer and empty packets in the trash.

"I don't drink...coffee." I leaned against the counter, still feeling the languid heaviness in my limbs which meant the sun was still up. "It's too early to leave. Not sunset yet."

"I know. But I figured It'd be nice to have coffee without all the estrogen." Tony smirked. "Your client's there with some female friends."

"I'll be good to go by the time you finish that." I glanced at the coffee, glad he'd poured it. Eating and drinking regular food worked, but all tastes paled in comparison to scent. Being a vampire was sort of like having a slightly burnt tongue all the time unless blood was on the menu.

"Figured as much." He splashed cream into his cup, making clouds in his coffee. "I got a question for you."

"Go ahead." I hoped he didn't have a terminally ill relative. That kind of thing was always awkward. Turning had strict regulations, and it didn't get rid of the effects of most diseases the body couldn't eventually heal on its own. Turn someone with stomach cancer, they'd be in pain for eternity. Turn someone with Alzheimer's, they'd never recover their lost memories.

"Why are you even here?" He blew on his coffee. "At school, I mean. Don't want to get metaphysical this early in the day."

"I need a license if I want to keep my business." It was mostly that simple, although I could have just gone to community classes. But I knew the Headmistress here and she'd arranged a scholarship.

"Yeah, I've heard that. But how do you still take clients?" He sipped the hot beverage, glancing up at me over the rim of the cup.

"They can't stop me from doing piecework, but the law says I can't advertise or claim any business expenses." I shrugged. Even with Extrahumans added in, tax law was boring.

"Fred's dad didn't have to get a degree to keep running Redford Renovations." Tony raised an eyebrow. "Uses magic and enhanced materials, too. Unfair, huh?"

"It is." I grinned, trying to lighten the mood. "I can handle it."

"Seems lame. I mean, you're a vampire and a Psychic which means double limits. You can't go out in the daytime, and you're a one-trick pony. Fred's dad is a full member of the Goblin King's court, with a pretty high rank. Redcaps are bad-asses. Way more there for them to worry about."

"You know an awful lot about this stuff for a freshman cat shifter." Redford Renovations had big connections, which went a long way in Rhode Island as far as licensing goes. Being Unseelie just made him more powerful. The King's power grew with every new changeling who tithed to him, and Unseelie was the way to go since the Extrahuman status quo changed with the Big Reveal.

Tony laughed so hard he would have spilled his coffee if it wasn't already half gone. He took a deep breath, then shook his head and ran a hand through his hair.

"School of hard knocks." He sipped. "I was an employee. Took two years off after high school to work there and save money. Also, I'm more curious than the average cat."

"So I've seen." It was my turn to chuckle.

Tony's mouth stretched into a flat line. He crossed his arms and tilted his chin slightly up, a hard glint in his narrowed eyes. His coffee stuck out in the hand under his left elbow, still upright.

"Not in a Psychic way, man." I sighed.

"It's not you, Henry." Tony's voice came slightly muffled through his clenched jaw. "Turn your ears up and have a listen. Someone's trying to break in here."

I tilted my head and focused my minimal daylight energy on amping up my hearing. I heard scratches and splintering wood. Someone was almost through one of the walls in the stacks directly across from where we stood. If they broke through, I'd be standing right in the last light of the sun.

I would have leaped out of the way, but the best I could do was a trot. I was slower than a regular human in the daytime, even with one of my senses enhanced. Tony did better. He sprang off in a burst of Extrahuman speed. Then, he leaned forward and rushed me. I hit the opposite wall underneath the mezzanine.

"Blanket!" I glanced up at the emergency box on the wall above my head.

"On it!" Tony shattered its glass front, then pulled out the leaden tarp inside and covered me with it.

I huddled under a safety blanket for the thirteenth time in my unlife, wondering how one cat shifter could protect me from whoever wanted me dead bad enough to literally tear down a wall in the magically warded Nocturnal Lounge. That took raw physical power and strong magic. I thought I'd have just a few seconds, but time stretched on.

I breathed to measure its passage, hearing more splintering crunches, shattering glass, and the noise of upholstery being torn. Some sounds were less than a yard away. Who or whatever had burst in was literally tearing the place apart looking for me. I had no idea how the attacker didn't see the bright red blanket.

After four minutes, the effects of the sun vanished. I leaped up, throwing the blanket aside to see a snarling jet-black form in the middle of the room. Wisps of dark smoke or soot curled up from its ears, tail, and claws. It went on four legs but wasn't shaped like any natural or magical animal I'd seen. Its mouth was pitch-black, too, its roar a hollow sound more like wind through an alley than anything living. It had no eyes, only emptiness where they should be.

Tony stood next to me, staring at the thing. He didn't move, and the thing didn't seem to see him. Tony slowly raised his arm, pressing a single finger to his lips. I didn't dare open my mouth. Magic. How in all the Realms did a cat shifter know how to cast a spell? I held my tongue, watching and waiting. And Remembering.

The best way to counter an unknown creature like this was to make a Psychic impression. I could erase regular memories, but not an impression. I'd never forget this particular attack for the rest of my nights, but an impression would let me find out what this thing was and how to stop it if it showed up again. Even better, I'd be able to share the experience with others as though they'd been there. I could get help as long as I could find willing people . Most just avoided vampires like me.

I watched the thing sniff Tony's fallen coffee cup, then the spot on the floor where I'd been standing. It raised its head to nose the counter-top, then followed my scent back up the steps and around to my usual table in the mezzanine. Its footsteps made no sound at all, but trails and tendrils of shadow clung to the spots where it placed its feet. Those shadows rose and dissipated in moments. Maybe a Magus would still be able to see them, but I was just a psychic.

I saw Tony shake his head, pressing his finger even more firmly over his lips. Overhead, a crash and howl carried down to meet our ears. Scattering paper and sharp cracks echoed through the wrecked Lounge. For a creature that seemed insubstantial, it sure did a lot of damage.

I breathed again to mark the time, straining to hear anything or anyone outside the breach in the wall. Normal traffic sounds from Thayer Street came through, plus the bleat of a siren further down College Hill. After another minute, I couldn't hear the creature anymore. Tony kept his hand over his mouth but beckoned with the other. Then, he went up the stairs to the regular exit. I followed but looked over my shoulder at the hole in the wall. I made an impression of that and the completely decimated corner I used to work at. Almost nothing was where it had been before the attack.

Tony increased his pace once we got outside, still gesturing for quiet. He led me down Thayer, then across to the dining hall. He went around to the back of the building and ducked behind a dumpster. After that, he snapped his fingers. I watched a parti-colored translucent membrane appear and then pop like a soap bubble. I remembered from a summer afternoon over forty-five years earlier.

"We need to talk now." Tony stepped back out from behind the dumpster but stopped at the corner of the building. He put his hands on his hips, elbows pushing the sides of his trench-coat out to either side. "I just saved your life. Not a peep about how I did it to anyone."

"You have my word." I followed him, watching his shoulders and gait ease into their usual relaxed tilt. "How did you do it? I've never heard of a cat shifter with magic before."

"How'd I do what?" He stared at me, unblinking. "Make up whatever story you want, but keep it to yourself."

"Do you have any idea what that thing was?"

"Grim." He dropped his arms to the side, looking tired out all of a sudden.

"Well, yes." I rolled my eyes. Tony, like most cat shifters, was frustratingly dodgy when asked a direct question. "That's a decent adjective to use for it, but—"

"No. That thing's called a Grim, an elemental, summoned, Pure Faerie creature." Tony turned his head to look me in the eye as he opened the door to the dining hall. "They'll be back two more times." He stepped into the vestibule, then went through the second door.

"Well, that's not so bad." I followed him, glancing around the dining hall to see a trio of girls at a table in the corner. One of them looked familiar.

"Oh, yes, it is." Tony shut his eyes. "Every time Grims show up, they kill someone."

Before I could say anything about neither of us dying, the familiar-looking girl stood up and waved at us. It was Lynn Frampton, mate of the bear shifter I'd helped just before Fall exams.

"Hi, Henry! " She sounded much cheerier than usual. "Happy Winter Inter-session!"

She had no idea. Then again, I barely did. All I knew was, things sure hadn't started out happy.

CHAPTER TWO

Maddie

I'd sat with Lynn and Olivia, having coffee and giving the re-hash of who I was and why I was there. Re-run introductions were boring but essential. Nobody except my immediate family remembered me because of Umbral Affinity, the lamest magus enhancement ever. Lynn was my roommate, so her memory caught up with a bunch of the things I had to tell over again, but Olivia didn't. She kept apologizing about side-effects from the medication to keep her on a diurnal schedule.

"Seriously, I'm cool with repeating myself." I curled my nearly always cold hands around the hot porcelain of the cup. "It's just part of being me."

"I just didn't want to be rude, is all. I should remember, too, with my photographic memory." Olivia twirled a shiny teaspoon in her already empty cup. "If it were me everyone forgot all the time, I don't know what I'd do."

"It's not rude, it's magic." Lynn had a book as usual. She read out of it. "An enhancement to Magi of the Umbral school, Umbral Affinity is the tendency to escape memorability."

My roommate closed the book and looked up. Her face lit up a little, but I knew whoever had arrived wasn't her mate Bobby. That would have made her eyes brighter than a Christmas tree. I watched her call out to Henry and Tony, waving them over. I didn't bother turning around, just shuffled my chair over to make room for them.

A strange tingle came from my right side as they sat down. I looked out the corner of my eye, wondering why Henry Baxter, the Psychic memory vampire, felt like Umbral magic. I turned in my seat to scrutinize any residual energy traces. Anyone who'd been around a spell in action or a magical creature had them.

His gaze met mine only briefly, then he cut his eyes away. I saw wispy traces of shadow no one else at the table could sense except maybe by smell. Bright scraps of some other magic I couldn't identify shimmered, fading just as rapidly. Under that, the gray static hum of unliving vampiric energy made a constant yet faintly pleasant drone. I couldn't find a trace of Henry's Psychic energy, which was normal with a side of regular sauce. Only dragon shifters and Tanuki saw both kinds. Magi like me needed a magipsychic device to get a look at that.

"So where's your roommate, Lynn?"

I couldn't help it. I laughed. Henry turned to look at me again, startling slightly so his mouth opened and I could see the tips of his fangs. I smiled back. My dad had been turned when I was little. Plus, I'm a little desensitized to anything dangerous. I'd grown up with an inherent fearlessness that comes from no one remembering who I am.

There were a few exceptions, but unless my own family decided to go on a rampage, I'd be safe from just about anyone or anything besides Pure Faerie creatures or natural disasters. And if a Magus with Umbral affinity ever went rogue, anyone they wanted dead was a goner, anyway. No one would see or remember them coming until it was too late.

All those thoughts happened in an instant before I was conscious of taking one breath. In the next, I noticed everyone staring at me. Tony was across from me next to Olivia. Both of them wrinkled their noses as though they both smelled something strong at the same time. I glanced back at Henry's face only to find myself eye-locked with him. Vampires don't have to blink, but he did.

"I'm Lynn's roommate, Maddie. Before you forget me again, I have to ask why you and Tony are covered with Umbral energy."

"That's not important." Henry kept looking at me right along with everyone else. I was a little south of comfortable.

"It is." I didn't want to blink, so I used the trick Mother had taught me and narrowed my eyes, then glanced up. "I'm not letting you do the Psychic wooj on me until I know you didn't tangle with anyone I'm related to."

Henry sighed. I could tell he didn't want to deal with this, and I felt a little bad. He probably thought this was more discrimination, and that maybe I was a bigot. Circumstances during the Big Reveal had caused a rift between vampires and the rest of Extrahuman society. I'd heard the humans were even worse.

"We had a brush with a Grim about fifteen minutes ago," Tony answered. "You want proof, head over to what's left of the Nocturnal Lounge."

"There won't be proof." Lynn twirled a pencil against a blank page in her notebook. "This happened at sunset, right?"

"Before, actually." Henry gazed into my eyes, but I got the feeling he wasn't just seeing me. He was Remembering. "About five minutes between when it broke through and sunset."

"Even worse, then." Lynn's pencil scratched more purposefully against the paper. "There won't be any evidence it was a Grim. All the Umbral residue will vanish into the ether in a couple minutes. Heck, they might even try to blame you guys for all the mess if you're there before the authorities."

"Even worse, the Campus Police probably won't do much." Olivia leaned her chin on her hand. "They don't care much for nocturnal anything, just like the regular police."

"Yeah, cops sure like to overlook things like that. But I have a string I could pull." Tony leaned back in his chair. "A Grim is serious business. I'll need some kind of proof I can show my contact, though."

"I'm proof. I did my psychic 'wooj' back at the lounge." One corner of Henry's mouth tilted up, but the smile didn't touch his eyes. "Is your friend the type of person who'd listen to a vampire?"

"He wouldn't even let you try to prove anything without someone trustworthy vouching for you, a description I don't fit, by the way." Tony didn't meet anyone's eyes. "He's a werewolf."

Hisses, boos, and even an outraged choke came from everyone around the table. Only Henry and I kept quiet. No respectable werewolf would believe a vampire about anything nowadays. They'd been the most at odds during the Big Reveal exactly because they'd been the most friendly before. Alliances going back centuries had crumbled when old friends sold each other out to save their own skins. I wasn't sure how bad things had gotten, but the only groups with more enmity were the two Faerie courts.

"Would he listen to Blaine?" Henry raised an eyebrow.

"Oh, definitely." Tony smiled, then let out a chuckle. "If you can convince a paranoid dragon shifter to head over here when he doesn't have to."

"Blaine owes me a favor, remember?" Henry folded his hands together, leaning back in his chair.

"He's over in Newport for Winter Break, but said he'd give dragonish help on the phone." Lynn pulled out her phone. "If Henry's calling in his favor, he'll have to show his scaly face."

I saw Lynn get up and walk away with her phone, watching her face brighten as her friend picked up on the other end. Olivia stared almost blankly, probably because of the Adderal forcing her into a diurnal pattern. I couldn't tell where Tony's attention went, but cat shifters couldn't resist eavesdropping. Henry turned his head toward the exit, then glanced back at me.

"If you want to wait until this is settled before I bind your amulet, Maddie, I understand." He put his hand in his pocket, then opened it to reveal what looked like a brass pocket watch on a chain. I didn't care one bit about that.

"How did you remember me?" No one did without a reminder once they'd looked away. I'd need to join a shifter pack, make friends with Faeries, or have a baby for someone to know who I was. He'd forgotten me earlier. But what if that had been an act? Vampires couldn't turn shifters or Tithed Faeries. I couldn't hide my shiver. At least Henry was the only one paying enough attention to notice.

"It's what I do, this Psychic memory thing." He glanced at the amulet in his hand. "I made a psychic impression, just like I did with the Grim. I'll never forget you now."

"Did anyone ever tell you making Psychic impressions of girls who were born after you got turned is a bit creepy?" I winked. What was wrong with me? I'd gone from freaking out to making jokes in less than twenty seconds.

"People tell me vampires are creepy a hundred different ways every day." He leaned his elbow on the table. "If I let it bother me, I'd stay home even more than I already do."

"I wasn't saying it to bother you." I felt like a total twit with no idea why I should care that much about what a guy I'd just met thought of me. "Sorry."

"You were joking." He shrugged, grinning mildly. "Most aren't. They don't care if they bother a vampire." Henry shrugged. "Anyway, I figured it'd be better to remember a client with

Umbral Affinity. If you need another amulet, you won't have to explain yourself over and over."

"Makes sense." I shook my head to clear it of the banter. "Wait, you made a Psychic impression of the Grim? Is that the proof you were talking about?"

"Yup." He tapped his nose with one finger. "I can put it in a penny or something, let everyone have a look at it. They'll get a front-row seat to the Grims' performance of *Tear Down The Lounge* without any of the risk."

"If you can make amulets with impressions in them, then why worry about convincing a werewolf? Shouldn't the police just believe something like that?"

"That's a logical way to think about it. Problem is, distrust isn't so rational. Let me show you something." Henry pulled a phone and a touchscreen glove from his pocket. "The technically dead need these." He put the glove on his right hand, covering his thumb and first two fingers. Then he tapped and swiped the phone.

"I totally already know vampires can't just use a smartphone without those." I smiled. "You're not my first."

"No wonder you don't mind sitting at the Goth kid's table." He chuckled a little.

"I sit at any kind of table I want. No consequences, no regrets. I learn better when I see something up close and personal."

"Speaking of that, here." Henry handed his phone over. "I completely disagree with the website I'm showing you, but I think you'll understand my point and reasoning."

I blinked in near-disbelief at the page full of misinformation. The header had a motif of Nazi symbols, and the sidebar's lettering stood out against an old, grainy photo of people in pointy white hoods. This was a website for a white human supremacist group. One "article" on this page refuted the Holocaust. Further down the page was a baldly revisionist five-paragraph "essay" legitimizing slavery. The last one told how vampires were just the gay people who'd died of AIDS in the 1980s and 90s, back from the dead to spread the disease. I checked the fine-print information at the bottom, hoping to see the tag-line of a satire blog. I didn't. The site's followers actually viewed the world this way.

"I can't. There are no words for this." I pushed the phone away like it was poisonous.

"I do." Henry took his phone and closed out of the browser. "Insulting. Sickening. Depressing. Terrifying."

"This problem of yours with the Grim will be tough to solve." Lynn's voice came from over my shoulder. "Blaine will help, but as you just showed…um, your friend here, most people will think a Grim hunting a vampire is the vampire's own fault."

"True story." Henry shrugged, then took off the glove and pocketed the phone. "Sad, but true."

"Jeez, sorry." Lynn walked around me and hunkered down to look at my face. "I definitely know you, but forgot your name again." She blushed a little.

"Maddie." Recognition made her eyes twinkle.

"Yes. My roommate." Lynn sighed, looking like she'd just scratched an itch on the inside of her skull. "Blaine and I will help Henry with this Grim problem. Bobby will, too, once he gets here. I can handle all the research we need, along with my termi-nology class. You other ladies don't have to worry about it."

"I'll help." I watched Henry start, and thought it was because he'd forgotten me. Then I remembered he couldn't. It was my turn to blush. "I wouldn't even be able to take this course if it wasn't for you, Henry."

"I'm in." Tony put his fists on his hips. "That Grim tore up the whole Nocturnal Lounge. I fracking love that place. Whoever summoned it deserves a piece of my mind and anything else we can bring against him."

"I'll help, too." Olivia crossed her arms over her chest. "I'm in the same class as Lynn, so we can study together and research Grims and Summoners."

"Great." Lynn stood up and stretched. "Let's hit the library. Blaine will meet us there. Grab books, notebooks, computers or whatever from wherever you stash them. I need a few things from our room. Maddie, are you cool with the Psychic wooj now?"

"Yes, but not here." I got up and shouldered my backpack. "This place feels like a fishbowl." I glanced at the wall of windows that made up the front of the dining hall. "Let's go to the fifth-floor lounge."

"Lead on." Henry put his hands in his jacket pockets. We headed out of the dining hall and over to the dorm.

CHAPTER THREE

Henry

I sat in the fifth floor common room, waiting for Maddie to come back from the restroom. I wasn't sure what got into me back at the dining hall, over-sharing with her like that. It had been years since I had a friend to talk to. Had I spilled my guts because no one would remember anything Maddie might say about me? No. I'd told her because her interest seemed genuine.

I wasn't sure how to feel about that. I'd always kept things like that disgusting website secret. There was something about Maddie. Of course, it could simply be the fact that I thought she was gorgeous. I hadn't been around a woman I'd found attractive since the Twentieth Century. She would have fit right in with the old crowd from before my turning.

I stopped reminiscing and got the amulet out again. I held it as though I could warm it even though that was impossible. Room-temperature was my default setting until I drank blood from a living creature. No one did that anymore unless it was a serious emergency. I'd kept my head down, played by the rules. Being a good little psychic vampire hadn't gotten me anywhere special. It also hadn't gotten me killed.

"Okay. I'm ready for all the wooj you can throw now." Maddie sat on the low coffee table between us. She held her hands out, palms up.

"Under the circumstances, do you think it's a good idea?" I stuck my hand in my pocket, fingertips brushing cold metal.

"It's the only idea. I can't do this lab without your amulet, Henry." She shrugged. "I guess you could let me fail if you're mean or something."

"But I had the amulet on me when I got attacked." I gripped the amulet, still hesitant to take it out of my pocket. "Had just finished it, in fact. Aren't you worried about the Grim?"

"Not really. They can't do anything to Magi with Umbral Affinity, you know." She smiled. "We always see them coming, and they have a hard time tracking us. Our magic smells too much like theirs."

"I didn't know that. Never learned much about anything besides my own abilities. I knew an Umbral Magus once, but back then everyone kept their powers secret."

"That's okay. I'm kind of odd because I like talking about magic. They won't be able to teach me anything about Umbral magic in particular. My parents say I could teach them a thing or five."

"Doesn't it bother you, that you're here to learn and it's not really relevant?" Maybe she felt the same way I did about being at school.

"I'm majoring in Magic Theory, and that's always relevant. I need to know how magic works because my parents are both Psychics. My aunt was the Magus." Maddie clenched her jaw so hard I heard her teeth grind. "She died when I was little. I'm mostly self-taught, so maybe that's why I want to be a teacher. Why in all the Realms am I telling you this? Oh, jeez, did I say that out loud?" Maggie's dusky complexion would have hidden the color in her cheeks, but no one can secretly blush around a vampire.

"Maybe for the same reason I showed you that website."

"Which is?" She leaned forward like I was about to put on some kind of performance.

"I have no idea." I held the amulet in my pocket, wondering whether a class was worth Maddie risking a Grim attack. "But that's okay."

"Coincidence?" She stared at my hidden hand, waiting for the not so big reveal.

"Not my area of expertise. That's a Magus thing unless I'm mistaken." I raised an eyebrow.

"Yes, and one I need this amulet of yours in order to study. I'll be happy to share what I learn, especially since Blaine still hasn't taken this class." She rolled her eyes. "Did you hear about his wacky conspiracy theory? He thinks some kooky Magi are messing with the school? It's truly tinfoil-hat worthy."

"Blaine's an overachiever." I pulled the amulet from my pocket, opening my hand. I wanted to help her. If the amulet put her in danger, I'd just have to help her more. "Also, not nearly as easy to talk to as some other people I've met."

"True story. Speaking of Trogdor the Burninator's imminent arrival, let's bind this amulet already." Her smile was easy and relaxed. "Lynn doesn't like being late to the library, whether she's meeting temperamental dragon shifters there or not."

"This binding will be a little different from most others I make. This is supposed to last three weeks of inter-session. You must turn it on and off yourself, so it's not running while you sleep or do anything you'd want Umbral Affinity for."

"Okay." The amulet could have been solid gold or a moon rock from the way Maddie looked at it.

"When you want to use the amulet, put it on, then say 'ex umbra in solem.' And when you want to shut the effects off, say 'ex *solem in umbra.*' If those phrases aren't okay for some reason, we can agree on something else. Just speak up now about it."

"No, that's fine. They don't use Latin in this class. Should be good."

"Great. So, when you're ready, just put your hands on the amulet. When I say the Latin mumbo-jumbo, repeat after me. I'll have to touch you the whole time. Is that all right?"

"You know, I was there when you did Bobby's binding." The little curve of her lips would have seemed shy if she hadn't been looking me right in the eyes.

"Oh?" I tried not to look as stunned as I felt. How she could be this calm around a "bloodthirsty vampire" was beyond my comprehension.

"Yeah. I know the drill. It's fine, I won't freak out about touching a vampire or anything." Her smile brightened until it put the moon to shame. "You're just a guy with a sun allergy on a liquid diet." She dropped me a wink, then took the amulet.

I had no idea what to say to any of that. If only being a vampire was that simple. She knew it wasn't. She'd seen the website and said I wasn't the first she'd met. Maddie had seen more than most anyone would imagine, too. Being effectively invisible meant she could watch or listen to just about anything without being noticed.

Any Magus with Umbral Affinity could walk unseen, hidden better than someone under Faerie Glamour. Some old legends said the sun couldn't penetrate a properly enhanced Umbral shield. I wrapped my hands around hers, feeling a slow, nervous fear that usually only plagued me in big crowds. I pushed it down since I had to focus. I looked straight ahead, meeting Maddie's deep-brown gaze. No, that wouldn't work. I cleared my throat, closing my eyes instead.

"This amulet will make Maddie May, Umbral magus, memorable while it's active. Those who encounter her for the next three weeks will remember her and previous interactions while it's working, even if they look away. Her name will be connected with her identity on coursework, and grades assigned will go on her record permanently. This amulet will cease to function when the Inter-session final grades are submitted, or after three weeks and one day, whichever is longer. *Ex umbra in solem, ex solem in umbra.*" I opened my eyes and let go of her hands. Maddie repeated the Latin with a much spiffier pronunciation than I'd ever managed.

"What did you do, go to some fancy prep school or something?" I clasped my hands together, not liking how they felt empty all of a sudden.

"Nope. Home-schooled." She peered at the amulet, then shrugged and undid the clasp on its chain. "Mom's a polyglot. I get all my languages from her, even the dead ones."

"How many do you know?" I was fascinated that someone this young had learned so much more than me.

"Only four." She slipped the amulet over her neck.

"Only? Most people just know one." I looked away as she tucked the bronze circle into her shirt.

"I have a lot of time to myself, whether I want it or not." She shrugged with one shoulder, the opposite corner of her mouth tilting up in a half-grin.

"Do you?" I was surprised. If I could walk around without people knowing I was a vampire, I'd be out all the time. It was dangerous to go alone as I was.

"Usually, it's fine that people forget." Maddie pulled her satchel's strap over her head to cross her body. "Sometimes, it's a giant pain. I learn tons, though, and that makes up for it."

"Bet that takes a lot of patience." I tried not to look too disappointed that we'd part company soon. I wanted to stay and talk longer. Instead, I held the door as we headed down the hall and toward the stairs.

"It's the very first thing I learned. That and recaps. I have to repeat myself every time I talk to someone." She chuckled. "Social interaction feels like the first minute of a Supernatural season finale."

"I hope you don't have Kansas singing Carry On Wayward Son stuck in your head every time." I smiled, , watching her curls bounce as she went down the steps ahead of me. "Do they ever get déjà vu?"

"Lynn sometimes does. We live together, plus she's super smart. Notices things." She pulled the door at the bottom of the stairwell open and held it for me. "It makes her more likely to realize something's wrong or missing."

"I know. She solved Bobby's hibernation problem when no one else could figure it out." I couldn't help smiling but turned my head in time to hide my fangs. "Outsmarted Blaine, even."

"Yeah. Blaine was spectacularly jealous. I watched him fuming outside the dining hall for almost twenty minutes straight, the night they met." Maddie's laugh rang out in the blandly decorated dorm foyer.

"Same night she met Bobby?" I wondered how she'd sound in the superior acoustic environment of the Nocturnal Lounge. Then I remembered that place was a total mess now and frowned. We pushed through the door to head for the library.

"Yup. And we know how that went." She sighed. "Cornily romantic, but it's nice to see people happy. Way too much of the opposite lately, you know?"

"Sometimes I think it's all I see. The downside. The clouds." I didn't dare tell her how much just being in her presence turned all that around for me. I'd sound like a psycho vampire instead of a psychic one. Bad news in the romance department.

"Means you'll be the first to recognize the silver lining when it shows up." She turned at the top of the library steps, standing at exactly my height. If the steps hadn't been so wide, I might have run right into her.

"Yeah. I think I will." I stepped around Maddie and opened the door to let her into the library.

Maddie gasped, then smiled as I held the door like she was savoring a piece of gourmet chocolate. Any chivalric gestures must be just as novel for her to receive as they were for me to give. Had I compared her smile to the moon before? Something other girls might roll their eyes at made her face glow like the last sunrise I'd seen. I didn't need to make another impression of Maddie May, but I did it anyway. Vampires like me had to take light where we could find it because we never knew when we'd see any again. At least my ability meant I'd never forget the singular beauty of that moment for the rest of my existence. The fact that a Summoner wanted me dead made any connection I could get that much more precious.

CHAPTER FOUR

Maddie

I'd had no one besides my mom and dad deliberately hold a door open for me. No one remembered to. As soon as their backs turned, people forgot. Blaming them would've been like holding a grudge against fish for swimming. In one of my many recaps with Lynn on this subject, she said I was too easygoing, and that I deserved better and should stand up for myself. I'd nodded and smiled, understanding that that was what worked for Lynn. It wouldn't for me. But that'd be different with everyone for the next few weeks, at least. And Henry would remember me forever.

I glanced back, a hot flush taking over my face. It was like having the flu last year, except my stomach felt fluttery instead of queasy. I'd read enough of Mom's corny romance novels to know what that was. I finally had my first crush. On a Psychic vampire who couldn't forget me. I'd talk to Lynn later about it, maybe more than once. For now, I headed toward the back of the library's ground floor, where my roommate usually studied.

A cloud of whitish smoke hung over the large table where they sat, a sign that we had a dragon. Lynn leaned against a sleepy-looking Bobby on a bench with a book in front of her. Tony sat on a backward chair with his arms crossed on top of the backrest. Smoke-rings wafted over Blaine's head as his fingers tapped out staccato beats on his laptop's keyboard. None of them looked up until Henry cleared his throat behind me.

"Henry?" Tony looked narrowed his eyes. "Why did you bring a random chick?"

I explained, resigned to an evening of recaps. But then I pressed pause and smiled so hard my face hurt. There's an amulet for that. It'd be worth using to stop a Grim from wreaking shadowy havoc on campus. I put my hand in my shirt, without a second thought for the raised eyebrows around the table.

"*Ex umbra in solem,*" I said. Then I sat down in a seat and pulled out a notebook.

"Excuse me?" Blaine peered over his screen, raising an eyebrow. Then he blinked and shook his head as though trying to clear it. "Woah. Trippy. Psychomagic."

"Huh." Henry peered at me too. "Yeah, the effect is a little odd, and I only see the psychic stuff."

"Lynn, why didn't you tell us your roommate could be a movie star?" Blaine might have had a sense of déjà vu, but likely no other indication he was repeating himself.

"I dunno. Maybe because she's fun and a more decent person than scaly playboys." Lynn rolled her eyes at Blaine, then stuck out her tongue and blew a raspberry in his general direction. Bobby laughed so hard he almost choked.

I laughed, too. That was my reaction whenever Blaine met me for the first time, so it did just fine this time. He shocked me by winking at Henry. The last time, he'd asked me on a date, then promptly forgot doing any such thing, which was fine by me. Blaine might be a dragon shifter, but he was more interested in the Extrahuman equivalent of Antiques Roadshow than breathing fire.

"So, Maddie here saw the Grim's energy." Henry's tone was all business. He'd leaned against one of the Reference shelves, hanging back from the others at the table.

"Makes sense." Lynn stuck a neon green flag to the page she'd been speed-reading. "I've got a book here that says they're Umbral creatures."

"If only we had a book on Umbral Affinity." Tony lifted the top book off the pile in front of him. "I thought I saw one around before, but can't remember where. Definitely not listed in the library."

"Nocturnal Lounge." Bobby stretched. "It hit Henry in the head the night I got my amulet last semester."

"Sounds right." Henry nodded. "Nice memory. Are you sure you're not a bit Psychic, Bobby? Most people just rationalize away the ghostly phenomena."

"I think some on my mom's side of the family. We get dreams about our…um, life changes." Bobby tucked a stray strand of hair behind Lynn's ear. She leaned her head on his shoulder and kept right on reading.

"Go look for it then, Cat Man." Blaine made a shooing gesture with one hand at Tony. "It's not like you're actually doing any reading."

"Nothing doing. I ain't going back there alone." Tony's voice lapsed back toward his classically nasal Rhode Island accent. He'd never remember telling me how he only did that when he was spooked. "What if it comes back?"

"It can't." I, at least, knew a thing or two about Grims. "They get summoned, kill, then vanish. They can't come back until the summoning magus calls them up again."

"Yeah and said Magus only gets to summon a Grim three times." Lynn probably knew a thing or three about Grims by now herself. "I'm still shaky on exactly how or with what. Everything

I'm reading says 'unspecified anchor material' and a bunch of jargon about Summoners. Summoning's Ph.D. material, you know."

"Well, if you're safe for the rest of the night, why not head on back to the Lounge and find that Umbral Affinity book?" Blaine waved his hand in Tony's general direction again. Tony homed in on it like a house-cat on a laser pointer.

"You don't have to be so bourgeoisie about it, Trogdor." Lynn rolled her eyes. "Jeez, I'll go."

"Nope. We need you here speed-reading." Henry turned, and I finally got a good look at the minimalist image in white paint on the back of his black leather jacket. I'd know that logo anywhere. "I'll go."

"Me too." I stood up. "If there's anything magic going on there, I'll sense it."

"It's dangerous to go alone. Take this." Lynn glanced up at me over the top of her book. She tossed me a pocket-sized notebook with a pencil stuck through the spiral binding.

"I love danger." I caught the dead tree parts and put them in my handbag. Even though she used computers like everyone else, Lynn believed in the power of tangible backup. I agreed. "I'll be sure and take plenty of notes if I see anything."

I trotted to catch up to Henry, who held the door again. That was so awesome! I slid down the rickety banister, almost twisting my ankle on a patch of black ice. I got a bit ahead of him, then turned around and started walking backward. I didn't care about the ice. The risk just made things more interesting. And I was about to kick risky business up another notch and flirt with a vampire. What was a little ice compared to that?

"Bauhaus, huh?" I gave him my biggest smile. "You paint that jacket yourself?"

"Yup." Henry covered his mouth with his hand, laughing behind it. "The foibles of youth. That's a lie. I repaint it every year or two."

"At least it's not The Cure." I stuck out my tongue, then winked. "I love them both."

"Only reason it's not is that I'm a lousy painter." Henry rolled his eyes at his self-deprecation. "Thanks for coming with me. Tony's." He shrugged.

"He seems more like a chicken shifter than a cat shifter tonight." I wondered whether cat shifters like Tony Gitano were the origin of the term "scaredy cat."

"Maybe, maybe not. A Grim's like a Great Dane on Umbral steroids. Can you blame him for being scared of one?"

"Not when you put it that way. Anyway, I didn't mean to insult your friend like some kind of nearly invisible mean girl. Sorry." I felt like a giant jerk, realizing I'd been running my mouth because I was nervous. Being alone with the only guy who'd actually be able to remember me was more than a little crazy-making.

"That's okay. Thanks for coming with me. I'm not used to having help, but there's a lot of that going around tonight for some reason." Henry glanced at me, his eyes meeting mine. I tried not to blush. It was probably nothing personal, anyway.

"Want to know a secret?" I glanced to either side, breaking eye contact while pretending to make sure no one else was listening.

"Always." Henry's voice was low and soft, not at all what I'd expected.

"You should get used to it. Bobby and Lynn are both convinced your wakefulness amulet saved her life last semester." I sighed. "If he hadn't had it, she'd be dead, and he'd have flunked out.

"Wait, what?" Henry stopped walking.

"You didn't know he used it when all that ice fell off the library and buried her?" I stepped in front of him, looking up at his face even though it was back-lit by the street light. "They're mated now. That's why he didn't hibernate. I thought you knew."

"No. I did not know that." He took a deep breath, then let it out slowly. "Did you hear about Blaine's theory?"

"Which one? He's got about seven at any given time." I smirked. "Lynn loves discussing Blaine's crazy theories. I've heard about them at least five times since I got here this afternoon."

"I'm talking about the one where he thinks some Magus manipulated the weather to make Bobby flunk out." Henry stepped to the side, then continued down Thayer Street.

"That'd be an Extramagus. Those are super-rare." I turned and trotted along to catch up to him. "And Bobby stayed awake, anyway. He passed."

"I know. But that's only half of Blaine's theory. He thinks the Magus wants to shut down PPC." Henry put his hands in his pockets, shivering a little even though vampires don't really feel the cold. "That'd be an insane Extramagus."

"Uh-huh." I shrugged. "More likely Blaine's dragon is showing off a little paranoia. They're known for that, after all."

"Maybe. But there've been some powerfully insane and insanely powerful Extramagi in Providence before. Partly because of all the Faerie gates in proximity to each other. One Extramagus got taken down when I was your age before the Big Reveal."

"Don't they all have to register now?" Everyone knew what the new laws said, even though plenty of people bent and broke them.

"Not all. Some got turned, went into hiding, or left the country. A few others went missing, presumed dead. Anyway, we're here." Henry turned a corner off Thayer Street.

The rounded entrance to the Trolley Tunnel framed a dark passageway. I faced forward and walked on eagerly. I never met a shadow I didn't like. My Umbral Affinity gave me a bit of night vision. Not as good as a nocturnal shifter's or a vampire's, but better than most people. The heels of Henry's boots struck pavement behind me as he trotted to catch up this time.

"Wait up, you'll go too far." He tugged at the sleeve of my jacket, stopping my advance. "The door's here." Henry's fist tapped hollowly against what looked like concrete but sounded like wood.

"Petrified?"

"Just so." After Henry finished knocking, a portion of the wall swung away from us. I saw stairs leading up. "It will be a mess in there, especially where that book kept falling on my head. The Grim annihilated that corner. But still it's worth a shot if it has information we need."

"Okay." I followed Henry up the stairs. The mezzanine was half full of splintered wood and torn up books. There were more stairs leading down to an area with old broken furniture. Broken was too kind a word for the state of those tables and chairs. Maybe they could be recycled into matches.

"Hi." A female voice came up from down in the mess we surveyed. "The Lounge is closed, I'm afraid. I should have put up a sign, but the ghosts needed me."

"That's okay, Bianca." Henry knew this lady. "Are they all right?"

"Mostly." A frazzled looking blonde woman with pink streaks in her hair stepped out from under one of the overhangs. If she was checking on the ghosts, she had to be a Psychic Medium. "I've still got a lot to do here, but I'm exhausted."

"Hey, I see an intact coffee pot down there." I pointed at the far end of the counter behind Bianca. I patted Henry's arm. "Go look for the book." I headed downstairs. "I'll get you a cup of Joe, Bianca."

"Oh, thanks." Bianca's dazed and weary smile spoke volumes. She'd thought only of the ghosts since she'd gotten here, not herself. "You're a lifesaver."

"Nope, but I have some of those in my bag if you want one." I grinned, rummaging in a low cabinet for a paper cup. No cream or sugar remained in the rubble, so I poured her coffee black. "Thanks, by the way."

"Horace here says I should be the one thanking you." Bianca gestured at what most people would think was an empty space to her left. "He says my aura looks like I need caffeine."

"You're definitely welcome. If it wasn't for Mediums like you, the poor ghosts would have some serious problems, especially after something like this. Do any of them know what happened here?"

"Not really. The sun got in, and the Skeleton Crew ghosts don't like that." Bianca sipped her coffee, then made a little smile.

"I still only know the most basic stuff about Mediumship." I glanced to her left where the ghost was supposed to be. "This must be awful, though."

"You still know more than a lot of other students here at PPC." Bianca squinted at me and blinked a few times. "What's that, Horace? Ah. A Magus. Most of you guys and many of the shifters don't understand what goes on with the ghosts here."

"Both my parents are Psychics, so I'm used to taking their word for things I can't see. But believe it or not, my roommate told me about the ghosts on staff here. She's human."

"Wow, far out." Bianca held up one finger, then glanced to her left again. "Hold on a minute. Horace says there's a problem—" A loud crash came from up in Henry's general direction. "Upstairs! Go!"

Bianca dropped her coffee and took off up the steps, her long tie-dye broomstick skirt flapping behind her. I'd gotten there before her, wondering what kind of trouble Henry might be in up there. Once I got a good look, I realized trouble had found him instead.

"Dahlia, stop!" Bianca stepped carefully past me and over chunks of plaster and wood splinters the length of her feet. One of those hovered in the air, Henry's heart directly in the path of the business end.

"Dahlia? You're the one who's been dropping books on me all semester? Please put the stake down." His hands were out in front of him, flat and outstretched with the palms up. "I only want to help catch whoever did this."

"What's going on?" I stepped between the makeshift stake and the only guy capable of noticing me for more than a few seconds. "Leave Henry alone."

The cool factor of my wannabe daring rescue attempt got completely ruined when I tripped over a thick, old book. I plucked the offending volume off the floor and sprang up, brandishing it against the makeshift levitating stake.

"Oh!" Bianca put both hands up to her face, covering her cheeks like that painting The Scream. The jagged wooden pointy thing clattered among the rest of the rubble on the floor. "Dahlia finished her unfinished business, just like that." Bianca snapped her fingers. "Last thing she said was, her grandma's book is in the right hands now."

I hefted the old tome, its canvas cover pitted and scarred by use and time. It had probably lost its dust jacket decades ago. I couldn't make out the worn words on the spine, so I flipped it open, turning past the flyleaf. The pleasantly dry and musky aroma combined with indented type and crisp, matte pages filled my senses.

"Well, we found it. Umbral Affinity and You." I turned around and held the book out to Henry.

"No. You keep it." He stuck his hands in his pockets. Henry strode over all the mess on the floor as though it couldn't trip him. "That's what she wanted."

"Who was Dahlia?" I scrambled after him, trying to walk where he did. Since he was taller, it was a lost cause.

"Another Umbral magus I knew a long time ago. We teamed

up with some other Extrahumans to stop one of those powerfully insane people I mentioned."

Henry picked up the piece of wood the ghost had almost staked him with. He pricked his finger with the tip, blinking. He dropped the huge splinter and his face twisted with pent up emotion.

"We got him, but she died. Her fiancé got sick, and I ended up like this." He grimaced, showing his fangs. "Coincidence sucks. Stay away, or it might happen to you." He hurried from what was left of the Nocturnal Lounge. I hesitated, glancing back at Bianca.

"Go. I'll talk to you some other time." Bianca waved the backs of her hands at me in a shooing gesture.

I nodded, not bothering to try to explain to Bianca that she wouldn't remember me next time. I had a vampire to catch. Coincidence made certain events more likely to repeat, but it couldn't be that absolute. Lynn had beaten that devil only two weeks earlier. I had to hope I could, too.

CHAPTER FIVE

Henry

My thoughts were in the past, remembering the night Dahlia died and the book found its way back to Providence with me. My feet were on auto-pilot, and I focused my hearing on the tinny Walkman headset's tones of Bela Lugosi's *Dead by Bauhaus*. I kept on walking down College Hill all the way to Weybosset Street. I headed further down into the city until the rattle and thud of a drum set and seriously amped-up bass guitar drowned out my music.

I turned left on Empire Street and stopped in front of a bank of flier-festooned windows. The chalkboard sandwich sign in front of the AS-220 billed a cover band, The Mission of Sisters. They were a Goth tribute, covering all the classic Post-Punk pioneers. I laughed so hard I coughed, leaning on one hand against the red brick between entrances. Irony was a church, this bitter laughter my solitary prayer. When I got some semblance of control over my hitching sides, I pulled a black cardboard pack of clove cigarettes from my jacket's inside pocket. My Zippo followed.

A flick and a puff sent me even further back in time. The memory shift was like the one time I'd been given morphine in the hospital, all leg-loosening wobble and white-cotton haze. Drugs didn't affect vampires unless we fed on someone inebriated enough to need medical attention. I didn't want or need them. Memory was my poison, the only substance I could use now.

With my eyes closed to the high-polished flat-ironed hairstyles and yoga pants as clubwear, I could almost pretend it was still 1985. The illusion would break the second I opened my eyes to find an empty wall instead of her and Neil leaning nearby, limbs a tangle of comfortable affection. Neil was a Null Magus, whose powers saw through and stopped other spells. He'd been the only one of our old circle to keep in touch after she died and I turned. Cancer had gotten him back in 2004. Nothing I remembered or imagined would ever bring them back.

I held the clove so loosely, I could barely feel the papery filter between my fingers. At first, I thought I'd dropped the cigarette. When a puff of smoke and unmistakable vapor of living breath met my nose, I knew better. I opened my eyes to see Maddie, of course. Her satchel bulged with the weight and breadth of the book Dahlia's ghost had entrusted to her. I wondered why she'd wanted Maddie to have it instead of her sister, Headmistress Thurston. She had no idea how heavy that book really was, and she shouldn't be carrying it. I should be nothing to her but some guy who helped her pass a class. I was dangerous, not just because I drank blood, but because of coincidence. She risked potentially fatal bad luck just by having me around.

"Sorry for stealing your smoky treat." She took another puff. "They remind me of home. Dad smokes these."

"He shouldn't. They'll kill him." I held out my hand, a wordless request to get my cigarette back.

"They can't." She shook her head, puffed again, then exhaled a stream of smoke through her nose. "He's a vampire, like you. Turned back when I was two."

"I'm sorry." I pulled the pack and the Zippo from my pocket, lighting up a replacement for the smoke she'd bummed.

"Why?" Maddie's gaze pinned me with frank curiosity, like a bug to a specimen card.

"All the natural and man-made restrictions. The world is cruel to vampires, with good reason." I stared back, wounded by her interest. If she wanted the truth, I'd give it to her. "Kind of sucks for your family, doesn't it?"

"Dad's worth it, dealing with all that." She turned her head to take another drag, but still managed to keep her eyes on mine the whole time. "Doesn't your family feel the same way?"

"I don't have a family anymore." Even though I barely whispered it, she heard my confession.

"I'm sorry."

"I'm not." Closing my eyes, I kept a tighter grip on my cigarette this time after taking a drag. "They're all in a better place than I am now."

"You have friends."

"Not so much." I opened my eyes, stared down into hers as though I could find what she meant in there.

"Tony, Bobby, Blaine, and Lynn are good people." She arched one eyebrow. "Even though I have to repeat myself every time we meet, I consider them friends. Why not you?"

"They could be if I let them. In the ever-popular words of Tony, 'Ain't happening.'"

"Fine. If the people busting their behinds to figure out how to stop a Summoner from trying to kill you aren't enough, what about me?" She stubbed out her cigarette on the wall, then tossed the butt in a can. "I went back to where you got attacked, then chased you halfway across town. Pretty friendly, huh?"

I had nothing to say to that. She'd stepped in front of a stake for me. I'd never really understood why anyone did that sort of thing. I froze up when things got dangerous, relying on the bravery of others. It wore me out. Maddie gazed up at me through a haze of smoke, her eyes shining between thick, dark lashes. I felt like I owed her an answer.

"Surgeon General says being my friend is hazardous to your health. The reason I don't have any from back in the day is that the ones who stuck around ended up dead." I took a drag, grimacing as I tasted filter. "The ones who ditched me went on to do very well for themselves."

"Hazardous friendship is better than none at all." She plucked the stubby butt from me, tamping it out and tossing it to join the one she'd finished. "And the last time I checked, you were the one getting attacked, not me."

"Grims go after anyone around. You saw what it did to the Lounge." I crossed my arms over my chest.

"It'd have a serious problem attacking a Magus with Umbral Affinity, even one as inexperienced as me." Her smile wasn't punctuated by fangs like mine but looked just as predatory. "Grims are pure shadow. I could hide from one for years, and with more study, I could eat one for breakfast. And if I had its Anchor, it'd be toast."

"Good point. But still. I drink the blood of the living. Not exactly a safe friend to have."

"Oh, please." She rolled her eyes. "I brought my dad his sundown pick-me-up until I left for school. No one sees me coming or remembers where I've been. If I wanted to, I'd be more dangerous than you. Next argument."

"I remember you." I slouched against the wall. "Always will. And there are other types of exceptions to your forgettable rule that could happen."

"Yeah, but I'm not likely to join a wolf shifter's pack or trade in the braniac roommate for a Faerie one. Even you wouldn't be able to see me when I'm hidden."

"Touché." I was still too depressed to smile, but I stood up straighter.

"Are they playing *This Corrosion?*" Maddie glanced over her shoulder at the chalked sign. "Suffering Shadows, they are!" She dug around in her bag.

"What are you doing?" I pushed off from the wall.

"Getting five bucks so I can pay the cover and go dance." Maddie pulled her hand out of her bag, gripping Lynn's notebook instead of a wallet. She dropped it back in and tried again.

"Stop that." I put my hand on her arm.

"I'm going in there and having fun while people can still see me, Henry." She stopped rummaging, blinking up at me. I could sense her blush even though I could barely see it.

"As you should." I held out my arm. "But I'm paying. It's the least I can do for someone who followed me all the way down here just to drag me out of my funk."

"No Funk. Post-Punk." She smiled and took my arm. I thought she felt feverish even through the thick leather of my jacket. We walked up to the entrance and through it, then past the bar and to the door leading into the venue. They asked for our ID, and I tried not to look too relieved to see them put a yellow plastic bracelet on Maddie's wrist. She was over twenty-one. At some point, I'd ask her why she started school so late, but now wasn't the time.

As we stepped into the dim room where the band played, she immediately moved to the music. I straightened my arm, letting her go to the middle of the space in front of the stage. I hadn't danced since the Twentieth Century. It'd take more than this to get me out on anything resembling a dance floor after all that time.

I headed off to the edges of the room, nearly running into the table with the band's merchandise on it. I picked up a card with a web address on it, shaking my head and musing. Even five years ago, they would have had stacks of CDs instead of cards with QR codes and coupons for downloads. I could read in the dark that they had both covers and original material available online. Maybe I'd check out some of their original music. They seemed to know and love the old-school stuff, and I had found nothing new I liked listening to in a long time. Even the campus band Night Creatures hadn't impressed me much. They sounded like Fall Out Boy.

After pocketing the card, I glanced up at the band. They looked more Emo than Goth, but that probably had more to do with their budget than tastes. This Corrosion ended, and I recognized the opening riff of *Swamp Thing* by The Chameleons. A head of riotously curly black hair turned. My eyes met Maddie's and her smile nearly blinded me, even in that dim room. I only closed my eyes for a second, and then I stepped across the invisible line that divides those who do from those who do not. I danced.

Decades fell away again. The only real difference I felt between past and present was the lack of an aridly fragrant stale smoke atmosphere between us and the drop-ceiling. I couldn't forget everything that came after the days I breathed for reasons besides speech or meditation, but I decided I'd take what I could get. Close was enough for me. My lips moved along with words I thought I'd worn out over the last thirty years.

This time, I was the one who made eye contact. She looked away first, but only as far away from my eyes as my lips. I glanced down to see hers moving, too. We lip-synced in unison about whether storms came or just showers.

The music took me and I spun on my heel, my body making movements nearly as automatic as the shapes of the lyrics on my lips. When I turned back again, I tried to find Maddie. She'd vanished. It wasn't just a trick of the light or an Umbral memory lapse. A spike of fresh and cold wintry air met my nose. It came from the back of the room. I followed it and found a door marked "Exit Only." I shouldered through.

It only took a moment for the red to overtake the edges of my vision. I had to get my blood-lust under control before I killed someone and got myself exposed to the sun. Rhode Island didn't have capital punishment, but people willing to "daylight" a vampire lived all over the world. They didn't care much about the laws on the books. Ironic that I had to watch every move I made while people like that got away with a slap on the wrist for murder.

The heady copper scent of human blood threatened to distract me as I dragged the rubberized nose clip out of my pocket. My Extrahuman sense of smell was always on, but not breathing wasn't enough to block out the scent of blood. Sometimes it was more like a curse than a special power.

I'd just about gotten myself under control, still following the anguishing and familiar blood scent. I focused on enhancing my hearing just in time to pick up a muffled cuss word. I stopped trying to move like a human and made a leap for the source of the sound. Rough brick walls whizzed past on either side until I landed five feet away from Maddie and the piece of shit who had her pinned against the wall.

"Your wallet's in here somewhere, freak." The mugger's free hand rummaged in her satchel.

"You're never finding it, bozo." I could barely believe my ears. Maddie' sounded more like an angry shifter than a frightened magus. "If I want, I can make it so you'll never find anything again."

I had no idea whether she was bluffing. My psychic powers had never leaned toward lie detection. I stepped closer, hissing and baring my fangs.

"You think your vampire pal's going to scare me?" The thief flipped his hand over, revealing a tattoo in the shape of a crucifix. His middle finger shot straight up in the air as though for good measure.

"Oh, give me a break." I rolled my eyes. "Really?" I pulled my arm back and curled my hand into a fist, ready to give the attacker a right hook. "After all this time, people still think that works? I'm Protestant, and fisticuffs never go out of style, pal."

"Don't you dare touch him. I won't be the reason you go to jail." Maddie's eyes flashed with deep, dark anger. And then, that deep darkness grew.

I had to step back to avoid it, but still, I peered toward them as the darkness emanating from Maddie's eyes enveloped them both. I heard a choked cry and then the staccato bass sound of sobbing. With my vampiric hearing, I knew right away that was the attacker.

The softly hollow click of chunky boot heels was the next sound I heard, then a murmur as she deactivated the amulet. A shadow emerged from the bruise-purple cloud of darkness at the end of the alley. Its shape sharpened and clarified into a petite feminine form. Maddie slipped her arm under mine, forcing me to either turn and leave with her or let go. I chose the former.

"I'm sorry." She adjusted her satchel strap on her shoulder. "I was trying to improve your night, but got the opposite result."

"I'm a little scared to say this to you right now, but you're wrong." If my heart could beat, it might have broken out of my chest just then.

"Oh?" Maddie glanced up at me.

"Yeah. This is the most interesting night I've had in decades." I grinned down at her.

"Interesting in the Confucian sense?" That eyebrow and one corner of her mouth tilted up in tandem.

"All that and a bag of Eastern philosophy." I let her escort me all the way up Empire Street to Weybosset. "Thanks, by the way."

"You're welcome, I guess." She pointed to the chain still hanging around her neck. "I thought I shut this off. Wearing it to go out dancing was probably a bad idea."

"How so?"

"I'm not used to watching my surroundings like that. I

thought that guy was marking someone else." A little rill of laughter escaped her throat. "I forgot I wasn't forgettable."

"Aren't you worried he'll want revenge or something?" I looked over my shoulder.

"Nah. He won't remember me." She shivered a little. I resisted the urge to put my arm around her.

"Wow." I walked on with her in silence, unable to come up with the right words until we passed The Arcade. "You weren't kidding about Umbral magic. If you're this competent, why bother with lab classes? The Headmistress would probably let you test out of those."

"I want to take them, learn more about Magic Theory first-hand, and see other schools of magic in action. I need to master control, too. I can only really use my powers when something's got me upset. That's sloppy, not competent."

"I understand."

"Of course, you do. It takes vampires at least two years to get a handle on things, right?"

"Even longer if they're on their own."

"Is that what happened to you?"

"Sort of." I wasn't sure how much I wanted to tell her. "Things were different before the Big Reveal. Some vampires back then thought it was a measure of strength to see how long the newly turned could fend for themselves. Kind of like free-range parent-ing, but completely different."

"Oh." Maddie gripped my arm tighter. I'd expected the oppo-site. "Dad had help the whole time."

"And of course, he had your mom to help him."

"Nope."

"Wait. So he's the Magus and then got turned."

"Guess again." Maddie's lips wore a smile, and her tone was still light. "Mom's a Psychic. Precog."

"Huh. I'm stumped."

"It's okay. My great-aunt was the one who inherited Grandma's powers, but she died before I was born. I've had no training at all. Grandma pissed off the Sidhe Queen. Some Seelie hound called a Spite ate most of her powers. She tried showing me a few little things, but I learned more from her books, to be honest."

"So that's why you're here at PPC."

"Exactamundo."

"Gesundheit."

Our laughter mingled all the way up College Hill. I walked her all the way to her dorm, reminding her to keep the amulet off until she needed to use it for class. She nodded, backing up on the steps outside the dorm until she was my height. Her smile was open, genuine. I hadn't even wanted to kiss anyone since last century. I couldn't stop myself and leaned in, brushing my lips lightly against hers.

Maddie ran her hands lightly down the back of my head, brushing through my hair before coming to rest gently on my shoulders. I wanted more from her than I could even imagine asking. The pricking of my fangs against the inside of my lower lip warned me not to let this go any further. I hadn't fed in over twenty-four hours and drinking from a human in public could get six months in prison.

I tried not to notice the way she watched my face when I mentioned I had to go home and get a drink but failed miserably. Maddie looked as hungry as I felt. Her disappointment was palpable as I excused myself for the rest of the evening. I ought to try to avoid her in the future, but I had one problem. The psychic impression I'd made of her was indelible. I'd never be able to forget Maddie May, no matter how much I wanted to or what I did.

CHAPTER SIX

Maddie

"Jeez, Maddie. What are you, hungover?" I hadn't heard my alarm going off until Lynn picked up my phone. "Get dressed and down to the dining hall stat or you won't make it to class on time."

Instead of turning off the chime blaring out from my phone, she dropped it next to my head on the pillow. I sat up and tapped the button on the screen to shut it down. Rubbing my eyes and yawning, I wondered why I felt so tired. I hadn't had time for a drink. Then, I remembered the mugger, and Henry kissing me. That worked on my drowsiness like intravenous coffee.

"Okay. All right. I'm going." I shuffled into my slippers and then to the door.

My bathroom basket sat where I always left it. The halls were empty, which made sense. Only Lynn, Olivia and I were on this floor over the break. So much hot water came from the pipes, it was almost a shame I had to shower so fast. After dressing, I slipped the amulet over my head, tucking it inside my shirt. It felt slightly cool and tingly against my skin, reminding me of Henry's lips on mine the night before. If I kept that line of thought up, I'd be too distracted to focus in class. I shook off the tactile memory, twisted my hair at the back of my head and clamped it down with a clip.

I headed to the dining hall, where Lynn was present as usual. There was just enough time to wave at her, grab coffee in a paper cup and buy a granola bar. I also snagged the holy trinity of dining hall fruit, tucking them away in my bag. The apple, banana, and orange would get me through as long as I could manage to eat them during whatever lunch break Professor Brodsky decided to give us.

The lab building was out by the gym over on Blackstone Valley Parkway. It was a way to go, but I liked walking. Watching people swerve out of my way and then scratch their bewildered heads afterward never got old. My feet crunching against the icy sidewalk ground out a counterpoint with the crispy breakfast bar between my teeth.

By the time I reached the PPC Magical Laboratory building, my coffee had cooled enough to chug. I gulped half down, then checked the room directory and my watch. My class was on the second floor, and I had five minutes. I took the stairs slowly, finishing my coffee at the top and tossing the cup in a bin. No one watched as I put my hand down my shirt and fingertips against the smooth bronze surface of the memory amulet.

"Ex umbra in solem," I murmured. Then, I opened the door to the lab and stepped inside.

Long, white tables met my eyes. They appeared to hover over the black and gray speckled terrazzo floors, but upon closer inspection, they sat on thick Plexiglas bases. The air in the lab had circulation, but the room was windowless. I looked all around for a fan and finally found one in each corner. They were half-circles on sticks, made of wood, glue, and white peacock feathers, swirling lazily on filaments so thin I could barely see them from the floor. Magical fans for a magical lab.

I took a seat at the front table closest to the door. Only the one in the back corner was occupied already. I never sat in the back because, usually, it helped the Professor to remember I'd just asked a question. Also, sitting closer helped me focus and keep my mind on the subject instead of whoever sat in front of me. I also liked being by the door, but that had nothing to do with study habits. I wasn't exactly sure where that habit came from, actually. Doorways are just so interesting. You never knew what might come through them.

A couple of guys showed up arm-in-arm, laughing together. They plunked their bags on the table front and center. One of them noticed me and smiled.

"Look at that. We won't be all alone up here." The one who'd spoken had olive skin, brown curly hair and horn-rimmed glasses over hazel eyes. He leaned toward me and stuck out his right hand. "I'm Ian, and this is my boyfriend, Charles."

"Maddie," I smiled and shook his hand. Once we let go, I waved at the purple-haired guy with the nose ring and blue eyes. "Hi, Charles."

"Hi." He pulled a workbook and some pencils out of his bag. Then, he blinked a few times and glanced back at me. "Have we met before?"

"Yup. Magus History with Feldercarb last semester." I smiled, relieved that this would be the last time I'd have to do a rerun with Charles for the entire inter-session.

"Huh. That was a big class. Sorry, I don't remember meeting you." He shrugged.

"Don't be. I'm Umbral."

"Oh, wow." Charles deliberately looked away and then turned back. "Woah. And you're Maddie from Magus History. Making me remember you is way advanced for this level of Magic Theory. Is it going to be a cakewalk or what?"

"Nope. I have a little help from a psychic, um, friend. An amulet. If I shut it off, you'll forget all about me."

"Hey, thanks for not saying 'again,' okay?" Charles chuckled. "Ian, can you believe this? We get to be in a class with an actual Umbral magus and remember her the whole time."

"That's awesome!" Ian smiled even more brightly. He opened his workbook. "Brodsky is fifty times tougher than Feldercarb. He gives quizzes before every class, and if you don't pass, you have to leave. They say he's harder on the students than the creatures he summons. Did you get to look over the material for the first class last night, Maddie?"

"Yes and no." I got my already marked up workbook out. "I read over it back at home. Spent most of yesterday on the bus and then did some other stuff with friends."

"You don't make friends with Umbral magi." I absolutely did not like the tone and timbre of the throaty voice coming from the back of the room. Still, I turned around before Charles or Ian did.

The person sitting in the back was rail thin and lanky, with glossy though unkempt black hair that looked surlier than what I could see of his or her face. I had no idea whether the owner of the voice was male or female, or what kind of magic they had either.

"And you are?" I wasn't scared of a surly classmate. Maybe I should be, but whatever.

"That's enough, Miss May, Miss Phillips." The voice came from the doorway. I glanced over my shoulder to see a woman with silver streaks in her chestnut hair adjusting bottle-green cat's-eye glasses over her gray eyes.

"Yes, ma'am." "Miss Phillips" sat up straight, her voice taking on a decidedly more feminine pitch and timbre. She sounded less antagonistic by leaps and bounds, too. I almost forgave her for being so blatantly insulting. Almost.

"Let's refrain from judging each other before we get acquainted." The woman paused on her way toward the front of the room, raising one ruddy eyebrow at the girl in the back of the room.

"Yeah, I'm sorry. Name's Nox." Nox ran one hand over her head, shuffling thick hair out of her eyes. "I was born without a wall between my inside and outside voices. It gets passed down in my family."

"Apology accepted." Almost doesn't count, but witty apologies do. "I know someone with a couple of sandbags where that wall should be." I shrugged. "I can handle knowing one more, I guess. Why not come and sit with me? The workbook says practically every project needs a partner."

"'Kay." Nox collected her workbook and backpack, then got up and sauntered over to the empty seat at my bench.

When I turned to face the front of the room, the middle-aged woman stood behind the high, white Professor's bench. She put down a clipboard and made four marks on whatever document graced its top. She glanced around again, then shrugged and smiled. Her teeth were just a tiny bit crooked and whiter than I expected for a woman going gray. She looked familiar, but I couldn't place where I'd seen her before. This was definitely not Pavlo Brodsky, the Professor who was supposed to be teaching Magic Theory Lab.

"Some of you may already know me, but I should introduce myself formally." She turned her back on us, uncapping a smelly dry-erase marker. The name she wrote on the whiteboard made Ian and Charles gasp almost in unison. I would have laughed at them, but was struck speechless by the three nouns: Henrietta Thurston, Headmistress.

"I'll be replacing Professor Brodsky for the duration of this course." Her grin was guarded but gentle. "He's gone on emergency leave, but don't think you're off the hook. Although I'll be running this lab more hands-on than he does, your workload will be every bit as intensive and hectic as you'd expect from him."

I raised my hand as she took four sheets of paper from the

bottom of the clipboard. She nodded at me but didn't speak until she'd passed all the papers out face-down.

"Yes, Miss May?"

"Should we refer to you as Headmistress or Professor, Ma'am?"

"Professor will do for the duration of this course." She turned the corner to get back behind her bench and sat down. Then, she pulled a deck of large cards out of her bag and shuffled them three times. "You have five minutes to complete the quiz. Go."

I bent my head over my paper, pencil flying. Lynn took all her tests in ink, but I wasn't that confident. Served me right for not being such a genius. Still, the three questions were easy. Most of it was common magical knowledge as well as common sense. I mean, if there was anyone in the class who didn't know psychics couldn't see magic, they probably shouldn't have gotten into PPC in the first place.

I was about to turn my quiz face down when I noticed my mistake. There was less than a minute on the clock, barely enough time to erase everything I'd written besides my name and the date. I blew wormy, pink eraser crumbs off the paper, so they marred the shiny white surface of the lab bench instead. Then, I flipped the page over and took a deep breath, trying to relax. I wondered whether anyone else had made the same initial mistake I did.

Professor Thurston's heels clicked solidly against the floor as she went around collecting everything. She spread the quizzes face-down, then turned one of her cards over in front of each finished test. They were Tarot cards. Mom had those, used them to see whether I was a magus or a psychic back when I was little. I recognized the Ace of Cups, the King of Pentacles, and the Page of Swords. The last card she turned over was The Tower reversed. Bad news, that one.

"One of these grades is not like the others." Professor Thurston tapped The Tower. "The quiz that got this card is the only one that either passed or failed." She turned over each of the quizzes after that. A series of blinking and brow furrowing got replaced by what I guessed was only a veneer of calm.

"Miss May, you passed. Everyone else did not. Don't worry, it's only worth two extra credit points." I heard the sound of one round-toed shoe tapping against the tile. "This will be the only quiz you get until next week, but its purpose was to make you remember the most important thing about magic. Follow the instructions."

"But how did we all fail? Those were such easy questions." Nox hadn't even raised her hand before speaking.

"Miss May, answer that please." Professor Thurston busied herself with corralling her cards.

"Right under where we put our names, there were two sentences. Instructions. Do you remember them?"

"Yeah. Something like that's on every test. 'Answer these questions in the time allowed' or whatever."

"Right." I cleared my throat. "But on this test, it said 'don't answer any of these questions in the time allowed' so we weren't supposed to write down anything besides our names and the date."

"Great Goblin's Garters." The way Nox said that was almost like how Blaine said Tiamat's Scales. I wondered what kind of magic Nox was packing and whether she'd been raised by Changelings, Faeries, or both.

"Magic Theory is all about the rules of magic, regardless of the course's unfortunate name." Professor Thurston shuffled her cards again. "You're not here to learn which theories are contested, have wiggle room, or memorize exceptions. You need to pay attention to the rules, how they affect spell instructions, learn them as though they're completely immutable. After that, you can start thinking about how all of them might still be up for debate."

"Is that why you flipped over Psychic cards even though you're a magus?" Ian lifted his chin off his folded hands.

"Yes and no." Professor Thurston stepped out from behind the bench, fanning the cards as she went. She held them out to me, and I took one. Then, she did the same for the other four students. "Psychics with Precognition use cards like these to predict things. Humans use them for the same purpose. They get oddly accurate results, coincidentally, according to most Extrahumans. But coincidence isn't just a fancy word for an accident. Each of you sees and manipulates magic, limited by your schools, just like the Psychics. Nox, put these on and tell me something about the energy on these cards."

"You didn't use any Psychic energy at all." She held the Professor's glasses up to her eyes, squinting through the lenses. "It's all magic around those cards. The only Psychic thing in this room is on Maddie." Nox pointed at me like the tallest toddler in the known universe.

"Yes. So, how did the cards predict that one test wasn't like the others if I'm not using a Psychic power?"

"That's easy." Charles leaned back in his chair. "Coincidence and magic are related. We're all magical, and that rubbed off on our papers with the graphite and ink. You tapped into magic, allowing coincidence to act like Psychic ability when you used the cards."

"Interesting idea, but that's not what the rules say. Hold on to that line of thinking for when you take Advanced Magic Theory, though, Charles." Professor Thurston nodded at Nox's raised hand.

"According to the reading from Chapter Two, you didn't use magic at all. You used the cards like a human would. Magic's everywhere, just like coincidences. The cards worked because they're around both those forces. The coincidence in Maddie's quiz pulled that reversed card to it like the moon pulls tides."

"Exactly." Professor Thurston got up, holding her tarot deck. "Now, look at your cards."

I blinked, bewildered to see The Tower again in front of me. This time, it wasn't reversed. I knew from Mom it was worse right-side up. I glanced over at my classmates. None of their cards were the same as earlier. Nox had The Fool. Charles had the Nine of Pentacles. Ian had the Nine of Cups. Out of the corner of my eye, I saw movement from Professor Thurston's direction. I looked up.

She held one hand over her mouth with the other on her breastbone. I caught a glimpse of the upturned card just before she swept it back into the deck. Ten of Swords. Another bad-news card. Actually the worst ever, according to Dad. Something horrible was in store for Headmistress Thurston, and if her readings used coincidence, it had something to do with this class. Then again, maybe it had already happened. With the Nocturnal Lounge trashed, she shouldn't be this surprised. But then, maybe she thought whatever was going on had passed by now.

I ran my fingertip down one side of the card. Not even a sting. These were some well-used cards. If the Professor did readings with them in the right place at the right times, she'd have a much better idea of the situation than a non-trad freshman like me. Unless someone was blocking her. That'd have to be someone who knew her well, practically intimately. I remembered Blaine's theory about the snowstorms and Lynn's icy adventure by the library last semester.

Professor Thurston collected the cards to begin her magical forces demonstration. I took one last look at The Tower before handing it back. The image of the two people falling from its parapet haunted me for the rest of the day. If Blaine was right about someone attacking the school, whoever helped Bobby and Lynn was next. Henry had given Bobby the amulet that let him save Lynn. I'd convinced Lynn to take a chance on making friends. The Grim attacked the Nocturnal Lounge. Blaine's next theoretical victim had to be Henry.

Maybe it was time to start taking Blaine's fears a bit more seriously. After all, it wasn't really paranoia if someone was actually out to get you. But the only person who believed the whole thing was Blaine. Lynn, Bobby, and Olivia had insane cramming to do, plus more research on the Grim and the Umbral book. Tony was on the crew fixing the Lounge. And Henry didn't answer my texts until Friday.

CHAPTER SEVEN

Henry

I sat in the PPC library boiler room the Friday after inter-session started, waiting to meet Tony's werewolf contact. It was dingy and dark, but at least dry and safe from the sun. I'd have preferred the Nocturnal Lounge, but it was still a wreck. They'd probably warded it, but with holes in the walls and ceiling, I couldn't go in until after sunset.

My building had a door in the basement leading into the watery tunnels under Providence. The only tunnel exits on campus were the from the Lounge and the Library. I heard the shouts and strikes of a construction crew from the former. It was Fred Redford and another gruff voice that had to be his dad.

The boiler room was all concrete walls and copper pipes. And the eponymous boiler, of course. It blasted out heat that made me feel like a cat in a room full of rocking chairs. At least if it malfunctioned leaking water would put me out if I caught fire. Still, boiling water was no fun even as a vampire.

I'd spent much of the day failing to sleep. I kept waking from a daymare I couldn't remember, which almost never happened. Most of my day terrors came from psychic impressions. There'd been plenty for my subconscious to choose from. The Big Reveal's survivors had all kinds of issues, from physical injuries to mental scars like General Anxiety Disorder, my own personal demon. And before you go asking, the existence of literal demons hasn't been proven by either the human or the Extrahuman community.

Finally, I got up mid-afternoon and pulled an all-dayer. I didn't bother feeding. We don't need blood unless we do something strenuous and specifically vampiric. I hadn't, and probably wouldn't need to do much more than amp up my hearing. That kind of thing barely made a dent in my reserves. Instead, I brewed up the last of my coffee.

I can always tell a vampire-friendly house by its aromatic potential. That and the fact that there's always at least one decently furnished sun-proof room. Nothing tastes good to a vampire except blood. Everything else tastes like paper. We have complex senses of smell, though, and coffee is one of the most calming scents to pick up. Another one is Earl Grey tea, which led to geeks everywhere wondering whether Captain Picard might have been a closeted vampire. I cleaned up, dressed, and gathered my things, sloshing some coffee into a travel mug to take with me.

It was a good thing I did. More than boilers and hot pipes made the library basement nerve-wracking. A crack under the stairwell door meant a scimitar of sunlight slid across the area next to the exit until twilight. I stayed way back near the tunnel entrance, which smelled almost unbearably musty. Everything down there had either that dank aroma or rust and steam.

The sword-like sunbeam had just started sheathing itself under the door when my phone beeped. It was Maddie, so I read it right away. I'd read all the texts she'd sent me about tarot cards and Blaine's crazy theories, too. I just didn't respond because it was better to avoid Maddie and keep her out of harm's way. The whole mess made me want to hibernate like a bear shifter until the problem resolved itself.

Need to talk. You up? I closed my eyes, intending to just ignore the message again. When I did, I remembered the soft heat of her lips against my own cold ones. That was strange. I hadn't made an impression of that kiss though I definitely should have. I pulled on my touch-screen glove and tapped out a reply.

Down, actually. Library boiler room.

There in 5.

I waited until I heard her footsteps on the stairs to go back in the tunnel even though I could smell whatever she wore that made her smell like jasmine and myrrh as soon as she walked into the library. That was a scent for sore olfactory nerves. Thinking of nerves had me fidgeting. I realized I'd been doing it since getting her message. What could she want now? She'd stopped texting about the cards and the theories on Wednesday.

"Henry?" I stood in the shadows, not daring to look up until I heard the door close behind her. The last thing I wanted was to be sun-blind the entire time and unable to see her.

"Maddie . What can I do for you?"

"I might be in a bit of trouble." The corners of her mouth turned down. I realized I missed the smile she'd worn most of the night we met.

"Meeting a vampire in a dark basement kind of trouble?" I stepped out of the shadows with my hands outstretched in my best Bela Lugosi imitation. Then, I waggled my eyebrows like John Belushi.

Her laughter echoed off the pipes. It was a little strained and frayed around the edges, but good to hear. I couldn't help but join in. The idea of a twenty-something woman getting my dated pop culture references was giggle material for sure.

"Olivia would say 'hoo, boy,' but I'm no owl shifter." She let out a satisfied sigh. "Thanks. I needed that."

"Thought you came here to talk, not laugh." I leaned in the tunnel doorway, knocked back by a wave of guilt. I should have at least answered her once. She'd been stressed all week over what was probably just a random tarot card. I'd have done anything to make up for it.

"I did." Her eyes roamed over everything in the room except my eyes. "Heard you're meeting Josh Dennison later. The wolf shifter."

"That's not what you're here about." I knew a subject change when I heard one.

"No, it isn't." She sighed, the smile vanishing from her face. "It's been a rough week."

"Is it your amulet?"

"Not really." Six of Maddie's steps took her across the small space. I knew the start of pacing when I saw it. "I mean, I think it might need a recharge before week three because I use it in the dining hall. Can you recharge it? Is that even a thing that's possible? How much does that cost, anyway? Do I have to call Mom or Dad for more money?"

"Maddie." I stepped closer to her, not just because I wanted to but because she looked like I felt, at the shoreline of a panic attack. "Don't talk about it yet if it's doing this to your nerves. You need to calm down first. Here."

I pushed the wooden crate I'd used as a chair closer to her. She sat down and gratefully looked up at me. After that, I heard her inhale, then count to five under her breath and let it out slowly. That was the same breathing exercise I did though I couldn't remember where I learned it.

"Maddie, you said your dad's Psychic?" Maybe talking about her family would help.

"Yeah. He's clairvoyant." She looked up again, her face calmer than before. "Jade scrying bowl is his weapon of choice."

"Wait. You're Shi May's daughter? I should have figured that out when you said your mom was a Precog." I felt like such an idiot. There was only one Psychic turned during the Great Reveal who used a jade bowl, and he had a Precognitive wife who figured out where he should use it to look. "Your family probably saved half the Extrahumans in the Northeast back in the 90s."

"Yup." She grimaced. "But now, you're the one changing the subject. I think Blaine's theory is right and your amulet helped Bobby save Lynn. You're the target, Henry."

"You believe Blaine?" I raised an eyebrow. The only thing most people believed about Blaine Harcourt was that he was loaded and a huge flirt. "But Blaine did tons to help Bobby. More than me."

"Right, but you got attacked." Maddie sat up straighter and folded her hands together so tightly her knuckles went nearly white. "Henry, it's been five days. The Grim can come back anytime. Maybe even right now."

"Oh. Well, that sucks. Maybe I should go home, tell Tony I'll meet him and Josh somewhere else."

"Look, I'm not sure the Grim's after you."

"Wait, what?" I blinked. "You think it's after Tony?"

"No. I think the Extramagus wants to mess with me, too. Hurting you would do that because..." Maddie blanched, shivering a little. She pulled the amulet out of her shirt like it was a last-ditch effort. "Well, never mind that. All week, weird things happened to me in class."

"Really? I've heard Brodsky's lab experiments are pretty tame."

"Except Brodsky's not teaching the class. It's the Headmistress."

"Okay, so what happened?"

"Professor Thurston uses Tarot as one of her coincidence demonstrations. I keep getting The Tower reversed and the Nine of Swords, and so does she. It's little things, but lots of them keep happening to both of us. I kept a tally." She pulled a sheet of paper out of her bag.

"Wait, are you sure it's nine? That's your tally?" I shook my head, handing the paper back to her. I wasn't sure how to tell her that I knew the Headmistress's unlucky number was nine. She'd lost her sister, and her aunt had gone missing on September 9, 1989.

She tucked the paper away, but before she could say anything else, the light under the door vanished utterly. I froze. Maddie turned, following my gaze. She gasped, then stepped in front of me. I was thinking she had a death wish or something.

"It's here."

I didn't need to ask what she meant. I grabbed her arm and ran down the tunnel at a fast but still human speed. But I couldn't do any of the vampiric stuff until the sun went down. Maddie followed. She had no choice with the panicked grip I had on her arm.

I heard the groaning of bending metal and splintering wood as the door caved in behind us. I didn't have to look back to know the Grim had come crashing through the door. My ears picked up claws screeching on metal and the hiss of escaping steam. I pushed Maddie ahead of me just in time. Wet heat blasted my back, hotter than a mortal could endure.

I bared my fangs, turned around, and planted my feet. After that, I screamed as daylight pierced my eyes. This time, Maddie dragged me away. Sun splotches danced in my line of vision.

"How did you get it to stop last time?"

"Hid." I almost said how but remembered my promise. I couldn't blow Tony's cover, even if I had no idea what it was actually for.

"Okay. Hush now." Maddie took a deep breath, then turned right. The floor sloped down, and the air got staler. She murmured the Latin to turn her amulet, off and the surrounding darkness got almost tangibly inkier. She clutched my hand in hers. I gripped back tightly.

She took two lefts. I couldn't tell her this new passage curved to the right without risking the Grim. She figured it out eventually. If we kept going this way, we'd end up in Water Place Park. At least it was January. Even so, the park would still be relatively crowded with downtown workers heading out for drinks on Thirsty Thursday.

I tugged her hand, slowing our pace. Maddie responded by stopping. I bumped into her this time. She might have thought I was waiting for the sun. It was down, but I needed to heal the steam burns. I could get arrested for having a fatal-looking wound in public. Yeah, there are laws against that. Since vampires are the only Extrahumans that happened to, it's a pretty bogus law. Still had to follow it.

I closed my eyes and focused on the welts on the back of my head and neck. The plus side to being scalded instead of burnt is your clothes survive. I stifled a groan at the idea of repainting the Bauhaus logo on my jacket. I was starting to hate Grims with the fiery passion of a million burning suns.

My injuries were worse than I'd thought. I also had to heal the sun-blindness. Those two things made me hungrier than I should be around the living. When Maddie turned around and looked up at me, I could see her clearly. Her mouth dropped open, making a little 'o' of concern.

I realized I had the impulse just after starting to act on it. I managed to stop leaning toward her with less than an inch to spare. She threw her arms around my neck and closed the distance herself. I put my arms around her, hands pressing against her back as firmly as I dared. She might be a powerful Magus, but she lived in a fragile mortal body. As our lips parted, I ran my hands up her back until one went on her shoulder and the other to the nape of her neck. Her hair was just as lush and soft as I'd imagined.

Last time I was this close to a living person while hungry, I'd intended to feed. Back then, that's what vampires did. After the Big Reveal, publicly feeding on anything living would get you jail time. They had a three-strikes system with a ban on concurrent sentencing. If I got caught kissing her, we'd be taken to the nearest hospital to determine blood-loss. If any was missing, they'd read me my rights.

I pulled away before anything illegal happened, but it was still too late. The scent of her enveloped me more completely than the shadows she'd drawn around us. I hadn't even focused and yet I'd somehow made the memory of her lips on mine as indelible as the first time I'd seen her smile. That loss of control was bad news.

She leaned her head against my chest. I wondered what she thought about the fact that no breath or heartbeat stirred within. Then, I remembered she said her dad got turned when she was barely more than a baby. I put my hand on her shoulder again. Maddie responded with a little sigh. I wasn't sure whether it was contentment or relief. One thing I did know was that the Grim had given up its chase by now.

"It's crowded out there, and I'm too hungry to be around people unless there's something legal to drink." I looked down to find her peering at me through her eyelashes.

"Luxe Burger has bags." She pulled back and took my hand again. "I know a shortcut."

She really must have a death wish if she'd spent last semester in these tunnels. I let Maddie lead me out of the passageway and through a narrow underpass. We came out just across from the restaurant. I still had to walk by people heading around Water Place Park and toward their pubs of choice, but knowing I'd get a drink soon helped me endure it.

The hostess took one look at me and seated us immediately. I figured she'd seen hungry vampires before. She leaned over and passed us our menus.

"I'll bring you a drink right away, Mr. Baxter." The low tone of empathy was the last thing I'd expected from a stranger.

"Um, thanks?" I blinked at the woman, watching her set a menu in front of Maddie.

"You don't recognize me because I was only eleven last time you saw me. Your amulet helped my Nana remember us all during her last five years." She clicked away, making a beeline for the bartender.

I rubbed my chin, remembering a pudgy blonde girl with pigtails clinging to the skirt of an old woman with kind but vacant eyes. Those eyes had sparked with recognition when I slipped the coin on its string over her head and activated it. She'd hugged the girl as they murmured pet names to each other. Maddie reached across, covering my hands with hers. The hostess set a filled hurricane glass complete with garnish on the table instead of the plastic cup and straw I expected at most restaurants.

"On the house," she said as I reached for my wallet.

She was gone before I took a sip. Another surprise; this wasn't animal blood. I looked over my shoulder to see the hostess toss a Rhode Island Blood Bank bag in the trash, human. The corners of my eyes stung. Having this kind of drink in a restaurant cost over fifty bucks.

"You went away for a moment." Maddie rubbed my thumb with hers. "You okay?"

"Better than I've been in ages." I smiled, not caring whether anyone could see my fangs. "Text Blaine and tell that skittish dragon to get down to campus. We're going to sit down with everyone, including Tony's friend, and figure this out. That Extramagus isn't getting either of us."

Even after the side-trip, we had a little time to kill. The walk back to campus was longer over land, but I didn't mind. She hadn't said a word about that kiss in the tunnel, but when I slipped my hand in hers as we left the restaurant, she gripped back. She hadn't looked at me like I was crazy, either. Maddie's hand was warm, of course, because mine was cold. I wondered whether she found that creepy or refreshing. Maybe she thought nothing of it in the cold winter air.

We went to the dining hall, looking for Lynn. That was where she'd said she'd be meeting Blaine. She wasn't there, but we saw Bobby in the food line. Maddie led me over to the table where he'd left his backpack and we sat. Apparently, she was hungry even though she hadn't ordered a burger earlier. Running from a Grim and an exploding boiler could do that. I wouldn't flatter myself by thinking it had anything to do with me. Then again, she was still holding my hand under the table.

"Well, crap." Maddie rested her head on her free hand as she looked out the window over my shoulder.

"Where?" I grimaced and lifted my foot, looking at the sole of my shoe. Yes, it was a bad joke. That kiss had me feeling awkward.

"Very funny. But not literal crap. Look at the library."

I turned my head, then sighed and covered my face with one hand. Another PPC building trashed because I was in it. Yellow and black saw-horses already barred the entrance. I saw Campus Police let Bianca the Psychic Medium in. Helper ghosts lived in the library, too. That girl was dedicated. I wondered what her story was. All mediums got their ability to commune with the other side via some near-fatal trauma.

"Well, there goes that idea for a meeting place." Bobby plunked a fully laden tray on the table between Maddie and me. The aroma of stuffed scrod and baked potatoes wafted up from the bear shifter's meal. I wished it was coffee. Fish hadn't even been something I liked smelling while human.

"So, now what?" I crossed my arms on the table.

"Blaine and Lynn will figure it out." Bobby speared a forkful of fish and chewed thoughtfully. "Hey, Henry? I just thought of something. With the library and the Lounge closed, doesn't that limit your daytime access to campus?"

"Yup." I sighed, feeling my eyebrows draw closer together. "Good thing I'm not taking inter-session classes."

"Still, it cuts you off from everyone." Bobby took another bite.

"I know." I stroked my chin. "Hmm. I wonder if that's been the whole point of the attacks all along?"

"Attacks? Don't you dare tell me it's plural now." All three of us watched Tony approach with a tall blond man with slicked-back hair. His posture was straight and bold, implying confidence that would outshine Blaine's bravado. He dressed in light colors like some kind of anti-Goth. Even his leather jacket was light gray.

"The ones on the Nocturnal Lounge and the Library, of course." Maddie looked him right in the face, staring daggers at him.

"Was afraid you'd say that." Tony shook his head.

"I'm calling them accidents until there's proof otherwise." The blond man crossed his arms over his chest.

"You'll get that soon enough, Josh." Tony leaned on the table. "So, where are we meeting now that the Library's off-limits?"

"Let me text Lynn." Bobby pulled out his phone and started tapping.

"Hey, I wanted to ask who's been fixing the Lounge? Same guys who are out there?"

"Yeah. That's why they're here already." Tony glanced out the window. "Redford Renovations. I worked forty hours already, and they don't want to pay overtime. Otherwise, I'd have to be there."

"Now, why does Redford sound familiar?" Bobby put his phone down on the table to wait for Lynn's reply.

"Fred. It's his dad's company." Tony waved. Maddie looked out the window. A guy in a red baseball cap waved back. I should have known the Redcap would want as much work as possible.

He was only a few more jobs away from being able to cover all four years of tuition at PPC.

"Oh." Bobby picked up his buzzing phone. "Lynn says to come to the dorm. Blaine can meet us there."

Bobby shoveled the last of his dinner into his mouth, then picked up his bag and the empty tray. He dropped that at the dish-washing window on the way out, the rest of us trailing along. This time, I kept my hands to myself.

CHAPTER EIGHT

Maddie

"So who are you, anyway?" I hadn't seen Josh shoulder into the space Henry had left between us.

"Maddie May."

"I've never seen you before," he said, shaking his head.

"Oh, yes, you have." I smiled like a packet of Sweet & Low.

"No way. I'd remember if I'd met you." His grin could have gone in the dictionary next to the word wolfish.

"Not a chance." I glanced past Josh to drop Henry a wink. "I'm Umbral."

"Leaping Luna, get out!"

"That's what we're doing." I stepped under Henry's arm as he held the door for us. Josh had to go around. He didn't look too happy about that.

"So, do you believe this story about a Grim?" He crossed his arms, stopping just inside the door.

"Yup. Saw them myself less than an hour ago." I smirked at

Josh's incredulous blinking. "I was in the library when they attacked and everything. And they trashed the heating system down in the basement." I walked down the hall, pausing to wave at Blaine, who was by the stairwell.

"Well, there's one good thing about another Grim attack, anyway." Henry's voice echoed down the hall.

"What could possibly be good about something like that?" Josh trotted to catch up with me.

"It can't attack again for another five days," Blaine answered, figuring out in seconds what it took Henry and me a whole conversation to grok.

"Any ideas on what the Grim is after, Trogdor?" Bobby punched Blaine in the arm.

"Two of them, actually. Maybe three." Blaine waved to Lynn, who was at the elevator. We all squished in and she pushed the button for the basement.

I found myself crammed in the back corner. I felt the weird stomach-hitching that comes with vertical movement, and then the elevator made a soft *bing*. The doors rolled back.

I hadn't been in the dorm basement before. There was laundry on the fifth floor where I lived and the odd hours I kept between diurnal and nocturnal classes meant they were always available when I needed them. Lynn led us to an old wooden door. She pulled out an equally old iron key and turned it in an antique brass lock. The doorknob was old fashioned with a big cut-glass grip. When Lynn opened the door, the whole crowd of us stood there for a few moments just staring.

The basement lounge was one of the few rooms on campus that hadn't been redone when Headmistress Thurston opened Admissions to anyone. Previously, only Magi and a few types of Psychics could apply to PPC. This was a room for them. I walked in first, feeling instantly at home in the space. All the wood paneling was real, not printed press-board from the 1970s and not whitewashed like the rest of the building. The floors were wood parquet, variegated boards making a meticulously laid herringbone pattern. Built-in shelving lined one wall even though all the books were old Reader's Digest condensed volumes. Six wing-back chairs sat in a semicircle with small tables between them. I chose the chair in the middle, opposite the door.

I watched as the others entered the room more sedately than I'd have expected. Even Josh looked around in clear fascination. I couldn't blame them. This room was like a time capsule, a look back at what PPC used to be like, beautiful and needlessly exclusive. I could see why there'd been some resistance in the magical community when Henrietta Thurston diversified the school, even though I thought she'd made the right call.

"How did you get the key, Lynn?" My question snapped her out of her reverie.

"Jeannie. She said we'd better respect this place like the antique it is." Lynn glanced at Josh.

"Yeah, yeah." Josh sat down near the door. "I know how to respect people, places, and things. I'm not the son of two Alphas for nothing, you know."

"Just quoting Jeannie." Lynn took the seat on my left.

"She's the RA." Bobby shrugged and sat next to her.

"For the rest of the year, at least." Blaine sat on the other side of the room.

"Sorry I'm late." Olivia stood in the doorway, a turquoise blue robe wrapped around her pajama-clad frame. Her platinum hair stood out starkly against it. Tony gestured at the seat he'd been about to take. She sat down, grinning up at him wearily.

"You're a real trooper, Olivia. Thanks." Tony sat by Blaine.

Henry shifted his weight from one foot to the other, then ambled over to the last available chair between Blaine and me. Once seated, he glanced at the dragon shifter instead of me.

"So Maddie, let me see this Umbral Affinity tome again." Blaine raised an eyebrow at me.

I pulled the book from my bag and watched Blaine's mouth stretch in a wide, toothy grin reminiscent of a crocodile. I waited until he grasped the binding before I let go. Henry pressed back in his seat as we passed the book.

"You had this with you in the library?" Blaine flipped through it absently.

"Yes. I've had it on me since you guys finished taking notes."

"Okay. Remember those ideas I mentioned outside?" Blaine's eyebrow quirked.

"Yeah."

"Okay. I'm brainstorming here." Blaine looked around the room. Lynn pulled out a notebook and nodded. Blaine nodded and continued. "The lounge got attacked. Tony and Henry were there. So were Maddie's amulet and this book." He patted it.

"Wow." Tony leaned forward, putting his elbows on his knees. "I didn't even think a Grim could be after an item."

"All by themselves, they're not." Blaine flipped to the back of the book. "But the book and the amulet aren't regular items. They've both got Psychic energy and Magic energy, plus some other things in common." He handed back the book.

"Of course." Henry ran a hand down his face, almost as though wiping away his neutral expression and replacing it with wan sadness. "Me, their owners, and an Extramagus."

"Tell us more, my fine fanged friend." Blaine leaned back in his seat.

"This book belonged to Dahlia, another Umbral Magus I knew. A group of us found out about an Extramagus who was trying to get turned so he could lose his magic limit. We were hiding the vampire he'd captured after some of our other friends broke him out. The Extramagus caught us, though. Dahlia died taking him out."

"Wait. I heard of a guy trying to rule the world right before the Big Reveal." Olivia shivered. "He was a nutcase. Read a little too much Lovecraft way too seriously if you ask me."

"Yes, same guy." Henry closed his eyes. "He could do any school of magic, but the more he mastered, the worse his asthma got. He'd spent twenty years tracking down the oldest, most powerful vampire he could find, then he kidnapped that vampire's wife to make him agree to the turning. She's who we rescued. Me, a Null Magus, an Air Magus, and Dahlia." Henry tapped his pinkie, his brow furrowed. "No, I guess there really were only four of us."

"There were only a few ways to get a binding contract back then." Tony shook his head. "It's one reason people don't like owing favors to Faeries."

"Yeah. He had a relative who'd just tithed to the Sidhe Queen sending ransom notes disguised as contracts back and forth."

"Wait. A Seelie backed this guy?" Josh's eyes went round and wide. He blinked.

"Yup." Henry sighed. "According to Extrahuman law at the time, everything was by the book. That's why the older Magi didn't help. Seelies love the Old Law."

"Are you serious? They wouldn't help stop Magus Mussolini?" Lynn leaned forward, nearly jumping out of her seat.

"You have to remember that not everyone thought Magi rule was a bad idea. Just a handful of us with nothing much to lose stood up to the guy. No respectable Magus would have dared break the Old Law like that." Henry sighed. "Times were different back then."

"You have a point, even if I'm not technically supposed to listen to it yet." Josh shrugged. "Whatever. I like a good story. Go on."

"Anyway," Henry continued, "After Dahlia died, I brought her book back here. Her fiancé, Neil, said it was what she wanted. Bequeathed in her will and everything. That's all I remember. But I didn't know it happened until Maddie got it back at the start of inter-session."

"So, I think whoever sent this Grim either wants the book, the amulet, or Henry." Blaine shrugged. "Maybe all three."

"But why send a Grim? Isn't that a little excessive and pointless considering how destructive they are?" Olivia scratched her head.

"The fact that it's a Grim just hints at a bigger picture." Blaine took a deep breath, then blew smoke trails out of his nose. "The stuff that happened last semester was excessive, too. Do all of you know about that?"

"I think I need a little filling in." Josh steepled his fingers and leaned back in his chair.

"Basically, someone dropped snow on Providence, and then a load of ice on my head." Lynn fluttered her hand in front of her. "I'm fine, thanks for asking."

"Wait. Someone can make a snowstorm and drop ice?" Josh's forehead crinkled.

"Has to be an Extramagus." I shook my index finger at his nose, pretending it was a rolled-up newspaper.

"Well, yeah." Now it was Josh's turn to scratch his head. "But aren't Magi one-trick ponies, like Psychics."

"We are, except when we're not." I winked. "An Extramagus can do more than one school, but there's always a drawback. An illness, or a limit on when or where they can use their extra powers."

"Like how the guy in Henry's story had asthma?" Josh rubbed his chin.

"Right." I nodded. "Most Extramagi are born that way. Usually, they come from families with a long line of different schools in the same family and a bit of Faerie or shifter blood thrown in for good measure."

"How many families are like that in Rhode Island?" Lynn had a pen and notebook out, ready to make a list.

"Hold on a minute there, brainiac." Blaine held up his hand. "It's an Extramagus with a PPC grudge. Magic families from all over sent their kids here. He or she could be from anywhere. That's not the best way to narrow it down."

"Well, how else then, Trogdor?" Lynn rolled her eyes.

"List magic families with Summoners, maybe?" Blaine smirked.

"It's not magic." Henry shook his head. "Summoning's Psychic. It's just the creatures they call that are magical, usually Pure Faerie."

"Back to square one, I guess." Bobby shrugged. "So the Extramagus can't even be calling the Grim."

"Hmm." I put the book back in my satchel and got up to pace. It always helped me think. "What about Mind magic? Doesn't work on Faeries, or long-term on shifters or Magi, but could an Extramagus control a Psychic?"

"You know, maybe one could." Blaine sat up straight. "I did a project on Mind magic artifacts. They were a thing back in ancient Greece."

"This sounds complicated." Olivia cradled her head in her hands. "Should we take this to Headmistress Thurston?"

"Probably. But again, it'd have to be someone she'd listen to. Like someone from Campus Police." Lynn leveled a glance at Josh that was almost a glare.

"Cool it, Frampton." Josh's lips twisted into something like the second-cousin of a grimace. "I'm sold. There's only one problem here. It's just a matter of finding something to convince my mom and dad."

"So you'll help?" Blaine grinned. "Tony owes me some money now."

"Yeah. I'll help you find something to help you with." He scratched stubble so light it was nearly invisible. "If you think Headmistress Thurston will believe you, go ahead and talk to her. I'd advise against telling her where you got your information from, though."

"Why? She seems approachable." I leaned on a bookcase.

"For you, maybe, since you're a student. If you can find a way to bring it up theoretically in class, go for it. But she clams up like crazy outside of a classroom setting.

"You know a lot about her." Bobby raised an eyebrow.

"She's my Godmother."

"Oh. Wow." Blaine rolled his eyes. "Someone here's an even more fortunate son than me. I might have a silver spoon, but Josh Dennison's got a magical Godmother."

"Please, no alpha-hole one-upmanship while I connect the dots." Lynn shook her head, scribbling down notes on her paper. "I need to hear myself think in here for about five minutes, mmmkay?"

"Whatever Lynn needs to get her brain in gear." Bobby leaned back in his chair.

The room was silent except for Lynn's pen. I felt something like a goose walking over my grave. The Grim couldn't attack again right after busting up the library. Still, something nagged at me like crazy. I glanced around. Henry spun a coin on a string. Bobby folded his hands over his belly. Olivia blinked at Tony, who peered at a speck of nothing just over my head. The toe of Josh's boot wiggled, as though he wanted to tap his foot but didn't dare piss Lynn off.

I shut my eyes, trying to focus my attention on whatever bugged me. It was behind and slightly to my right. I stood, keeping my eyes closed and felt my way along the bookshelves. The energy was close, but higher. I stood on my toes and reached up with my left arm. My fingertips traced a fine and fuzzy layer of dust. And then my touch met cold metal. I opened my eyes just as a brass oil lamp tipped off the shelf I'd knocked it from.

"Eek!" My arms flew above my head, making a circle. The lamp clanged to the floor. I heard a low, angry growl from Josh's direction.

"You okay?" Henry's voice was right in my ear.

I blinked, glancing around. I was on the opposite side of the room, looking at the entire half-circle of wingback chairs. Six pairs of eyes blinked at me, the faces housing them tilted up higher than usual to gaze at me. My feet dangled in thin air. Arms supported me under my shoulders and knees.

"Um, Henry?" Of course, it was Blaine opening his big mouth first. "Didn't your mother teach you that it's not a good idea to meddle in the affairs of Magi?"

"He's not meddling in my affairs." I cleared my throat, glancing from Henry's face to the ground. "He just kept that lamp from knocking me out."

Henry put me down. I smoothed out my skirt and straightened my top. I was less mussed than after our adventure in the tunnels earlier. Henry put his hands behind his back and stood up straight. He didn't move or even look at me. I didn't have to wonder why. Josh glared like a basilisk, his upper lip curled back in a sneer.

"Lamp?" Bobby blinked and looked around. "What lamp?" He wrinkled his nose. "Wait. I smell old oil."

"Yup." Tony got out of his chair and strode across the room to where I'd been. "This old thing was hiding up there on the shelf, I think." He pulled a long scarf out of his pocket and wrapped his hands before touching the lamp. Then he looked at me. "It's not dusty. You touched it. Well, crap."

"Yeah, but just barely." I looked down at my left hand. It seemed normal enough, no purple polka-dots or nails growing at an alarming rate. "Why? Is that a bad thing or something?"

"Maybe, maybe not." Tony shrugged. "You won't know until something weird happens."

"Awesome. Because nothing weird is already happening to me." I rolled my eyes. "What is that lamp, anyway?"

"Djinn house." Blaine peered at the lamp once Tony put it down on a table. "They're imprisoned Faeries."

"Are they, um." Bobby took a deep breath and looked around. "Seelie or Unseelie?"

"Dude, don't worry about saying either of those words around anyone here. None of us are in either of those Courts. It's all good." Tony shrugged.

"Oh. Okay, then."

"Anyway, there's no way to tell which flavor until the Djinn comes out. Which, hmm." Blaine examined the lamp. I watched ruddy scales cover his hands. He picked it up, turned it over, and shook it. The lid stayed affixed. "It's in service already. We can't even talk to this Djinn until either its term is up or whoever it's serving decides to fess up."

"Well, we should leave." Tony had packed up his things faster than I could track. "Put that damn lamp back on the shelf. We shouldn't talk around it."

"Wait, you think this lamp is spying on us?" Josh blinked, then turned his head to stare daggers at the lamp instead of the vamp.

"Better safe than sorry, especially since we're dealing with a Summoner." Blaine sighed and shook his head, getting up to return the lamp to the shelf. "My parents have the biggest hoard in this hemisphere, and even they don't want a Djinn's lamp. Too risky, according to Mother."

"Oh, for goodness' sake, let's just go already before Cat Man has kittens." Lynn waved her hand over a head still bent over her notebook. I recognized the beginning of her bossiest tone, which it seemed we needed just about then. "Trogdor's right. Olivia, go get some sleep. I'll have something for you to do tomorrow. And Blaine, can you go back to your parents' library? Make a list of things Summoners call up and send it along. All the Summoning books are on reserve all of a sudden."

"Will do." Blaine shouldered his backpack. He opened the door for Olivia, then followed her out. Tony watched them go, an inscrutably catlike expression on his face.

"I'm going to order a pizza." Bobby stood up and stretched. "We can have it in the first-floor lounge. By the time it gets here, we'll want a break."

"Maddie, I need to go upstairs and get more books. A lot of them." Lynn put her notebook and pen down on top of the already substantial stack of books. "Help a girl out."

"Sure thing." I followed her out of the room, realizing I'd be leaving Henry and Josh alone in there. Not the best idea, maybe, but it probably had to be done. Twenty years of bad-will between vampires and werewolves would just hang around like a rotten smell until they cleared the air.

The tension in the room was palpable as I reached out to shut the door behind me. The two men stared at each other, looking like negative images, dark-haired Henry clad all in black and blond Josh in a white t-shirt and acid-wash jeans. I hoped they wouldn't trash the room and give Jeannie a reason to go all bear-form on them once they got done with their chat.

CHAPTER NINE

Henry

"Okay, Wolfenstein, out with it." I had to tilt my head up just slightly to glare directly into Josh's eyes.

"You touch another mortal in my presence again, we will have a problem." He put his hands on his hips.

"I didn't see you rushing to help." I raised an eyebrow.

"Because Umbral Magi can take care of themselves. They don't need undead blood-drinkers putting their hands all over them to avoid getting hit in the head."

"You may be right." I couldn't shut off the internal Billy Joel soundtrack about how I may be crazy but it just may be a lunatic she was looking for. I did stop the smirk it inspired from touching my lips. "What's your problem with me, anyway? You don't freak out about the guys in Night Creatures."

"They were all turned near the end of the Big Reveal." Josh bared his teeth. "I know you've been operating much longer than that. How old are you anyway?"

"Not really that old. Turned in 1989." I held his gaze. In a staring match, vampires have a distinct advantage. Biologically , we don't need to blink. I'd made a habit of it, though, so it took a little focus.

"And how many did you turn in the 90s?"

"None."

"How about before and after that?"

"None."

"Bullshit. Vamps always want to turn someone. It's part of your biology, after all."

"Still, I haven't." I'd almost forgotten that Josh was a sophomore here at PPC. He'd probably taken some kind of Extrahuman Biology class by now. He'd know vampires can only reproduce either by turning people or mating with other vampires. The latter was a long and complicated process.

"How do you manage that when vampires much older than you went on a turning spree all over the world?"

"Because I never got into the business of making and pulling strings like the really old vampires. I was a Psychic first, back before basic focus training got integrated into regular schools. I learned how to control myself before you were even a twinkle in your mother's eye."

"Huh. Who trained you, then?" He raised an eyebrow, lifting his head so he could look down his nose at me.

"One of the best Psychics in Providence from back in the 60s." I hoped I was right. The identity of my mentor was something I must have put in the memory bank and then wiped.

"I don't suppose you have proof?"

"Ask Professor Watkins. He signs off on all my papers."

"He's a Projection Psychic, not the Memory kind." Josh's surly tone made me struggle against shooting back some old Star Trek quote at him.

I know. But he vouches for me all the same, and it's easy

enough for you to check. Are you going to argue with an old Navy Seal?"

"Fine. I'll believe you for now. But you have to admit you're pretty damn dangerous."

"So are you." I put my hands on my hips. "Do you need a lecture about all the Magi and Psychics you dated last semester?"

"I can control myself. My parents are Alphas who expect me to follow in their footsteps."

"Just like a vampire trying not to get arrested or, worse, has to control himself, or are wolf shifters deadlier than undead blood-drinkers?"

"Point taken." His concession came through clenched teeth, but the fact that it came at all told me Josh was probably more easy-going than typical Alpha heirs. I didn't have time to delve into the reason for that but made a mental note that it existed all the same.

"So, can we just agree to disagree now and focus on the truly creepy conspiracy theory that two out of two brainiacs agree on?"

"Not just yet. Still a hatchet to bury."

"And that is?"

"Maddie." Josh's lip curled again. I blinked, surprised he still remembered her after she'd left the room. The amulet would have lost its effect on him once she left. "Don't be so surprised I remember her. It's a wolfy Alpha thing. Memory Psychics aren't the only ones who can trump Umbral Affinity. Faerie magic can do it, too."

"Ah." I knew wolf Alphas remembered everyone in their packs. That meant either Maddie had wolf shifter blood some-where in her family history, or Josh was forming some kind of pack. That gave this conversation more weight than I'd initially thought. Maybe this was a dominance contest with Josh trying to protect a potential pack member or establish a pecking order. "So, what is the problem with Maddie, exactly?"

"Like I said, you're all over her. You spent time with her before this meeting. Alone time. Touchy-feely time." He narrowed his eyes. "Explain."

"We ran from the Grim together. It attacked us in the library basement, just like she said." I scoffed. "Thought you said you believed that."

"What else?" Josh would know if I lied. Wolf shifters could smell everything vampires could.

"She kissed me." I took a deep breath, trying not to lick my lips.

"Don't let her. You're no good for someone like her." He crossed his arms over his chest. "It's creepy for old vamps to hit on chicks more than half their age."

"You're right." I thought about the first time I saw her smile and how her first thought after the attack had been for me. Someone with that kind of light inside should never have to consider an eternity without the sun. I should back off and give her room to make her mind up about that.

"Huh." Now it was Josh's turn to blink. "So what are you going to do about it?"

"You're the big Alpha on campus here, Josh. I'm not challenging you on that. All I do is jog memories and give advice. You tell me. What should I do about it?"

"Stay away from her." He barked it like the order it was. No mere suggestion from the likes of Joshua Dennison.

"Can't really do that, since the Grim seems to be after both of us and we're all working on this Extramagus thing."

"Okay, you have a point." Josh glanced at the shelf with the Djinn lamp. "So, stop rushing to help her. Stop acting like Prince Charming when you're Count Dracula."

"Fine. I'll quit with anything that might remotely resemble flirting. I answered your question. She's like your pack-mate now, right? So what are you going to do about keeping her in check?"

"Shouldn't that be enough?" He raised an eyebrow.

"Nope." This time, I let the corners of my mouth tilt up. Giving in to Josh's play for dominance over the group had been freeing, lifted a huge weight off my shoulders. All the same, I wasn't going to play Omega. I'd call things as I saw them even when it wasn't what he wanted to hear.

"Why?"

"Because Maddie's strong-willed. And she's lonely. That's not something you're going to understand right away, so let me lay it out for you. She's spent most of her life with only her parents and maybe her grandparents able to remember her. When I gave her that amulet, she looked at it like salvation. Do you know the first thing she did once she had it?"

"No. Tell me."

"She followed me downtown and went to a concert." I looked him right in his reddish-brown eyes. I kept staring, not blinking or indicating in any way that my next admission felt like a knife to the gut. Josh had my support in taking control of the Grim situation. Now, I was about to put my chances with Maddie in his hands. It was the best thing I could do for her, the safest thing, what she deserved. "Right now, she thinks I'm the only guy who will remember her, ever. She doesn't care that I'm undead and dangerous and twice her age."

"Huh." Josh's lips stretched out in a wide grin that shifted into a bright smile. "I know exactly what to do about that." He ran a hand through his hair and popped his collar. "Thanks, Henry. You're not so bad. If all the vampires acted like you, there might be a chance at rebuilding the ties between our people."

I watched him turn on his heel and stride out of the room. If rolling over for an up-and-coming wolf Alpha would keep Maddie safe from the Grim, I'd do it a hundred times over. Maybe he'd even help protect me in the process. And as much as it'd hurt to watch Josh court the first girl I'd cared for since the Cold War, I knew it'd be less painful than watching her torn to pieces by the Grim or whatever else got summoned. She might end up rejecting him anyway, stubborn as she was.

There wasn't a future for someone like her with me. Her own parents were a testament to that. Her mother was still human even though her father had been a vampire for most of Maddie's life. The approvals board for turning was an endless nest of vipers disguised as red tape. If they hadn't given her parents approval, they'd be unlikely to grant it to her.

I shouldered the leather jacket that had been my only physical comfort for what seemed like forever. As I headed out of the room, I took one last look at the Djinn's lamp on the shelf. There was no way to tell whether it was already in use like Blaine and Tony had said. Still, it was tempting to go over and give it a rub, anyway. A few wishes might help us. But I couldn't risk it. The Djinn might serve the summoner. It also might be Unseelie, which would make its wishes more like something out of *The Monkey's Paw* than Disneyland.

I pressed the bottom button on the old-fashioned light-switch, then stepped out of the room. As the door closed behind me, I understood that another portal had shut during my earlier conversation with Josh. The saying about a door closing and a window opening was a crock of bull. Vampires were supposed to shut themselves up in lightless rooms after all. I'd have to just stick with my decision to do what was best for everyone. For Maddie, especially. I already cared too much.

CHAPTER TEN

Maddie

There wasn't much to do at the first-floor lounge. I watched the door for Henry, but only Josh appeared. He wolfed down slices of pepperoni pizza from Caserta's. Ha, "wolfed." I didn't blame him. It was good stuff. Blaine even took a few slices on the road back to Newport.

I listened to Lynn ask Tony way more than twenty questions. He described some other creatures that Summoners could bind. Seelie Brownies were physically weak but excellent spies. They could make bargains with either Unseelie Gnomes or the Seelie Imps who twisted time or made miracles. Pixies did everything through water, with Sprites their airy counterparts. Spites were Sprites morphed into Spectral hounds the Queen had made to counter the King's Grims. Spectral magic was the opposite of Umbral, like fire to water.

I wondered how a cat shifter had all this information about Faerie creatures. Lynn's left eyebrow would soon get stuck in the upright position if it hadn't already. I had a feeling she'd figure out what was up with Tony sooner or later.

Later on, Bobby and Lynn walked ahead of me toward our room. She went back down the hall with him after a murmured conversation I tried not to listen to. I went to bed, remembering those risky stolen moments with Henry. I'd been at his mercy, but he'd controlled himself. That had to mean something.

I gazed at the shadowy ceiling, reached out with one hand, made swirls and eddies in what everyone thought was the absence of light. Shadow play was the most common way Magi discovered their children had Umbral talent. Mom told a story of how she used to find shadowscapes above my crib. My earliest memories were of shadows and the other stories Mom told when she thought I wasn't listening. The sad one about how my aunt died alone because no one could remember her long enough to save her life. Would I end up like her, or like Grandma? Grandpa Joe was a wolf shifter, able to recall her because of their pack ties.

Eventually, sleep turned the shadows into dreams. My alarm went off what felt like a minute later. I got ready for class, then headed straight down to Thayer Street. I wanted to see my friends that morning but needed my thoughts more. The snow from before winter break had melted. It was weird to walk down streets with just an occasional dingy gray snow pile in January. In Vermont, the snow stuck around longer. I stopped at Au Bon Pain for a croissant since I'd skipped the dining hall. I relished the quiet anonymity of interacting with people who wouldn't remember me even with my amulet. The staff in the cafe had no idea a Summoner was messing with the school down the street.

I was used to Umbral Affinity for the daily minutiae of living. On a contemplative morning like this, activating the amulet to get breakfast would just make me feel like a falcon with wet wings. That reminded me to spend the rest of the walk thinking about my notes. There'd be a test at the end of class today.

I was ten minutes early, so I said the incantation to turn the amulet on before walking into the classroom. Charles and Ian were already there. They passed their notebooks back and forth, getting in some studying I'd neglected the night before. Being chased through the catacombs and then finding a Djinn lamp had put a monkey wrench in those plans. Last-minute studying seemed like a good idea.

"Do you mind some company?" I smiled as Charles and Ian looked up from their work.

"Drag a chair over." Ian waved at the empty end of the bench. "We're on device activation, figure it'd dovetail nicely with the activity today."

"Oh, yeah, we're making simple gadgets today." I pulled up a chair and sat.

"Have you ever done that?" Charles ran one hand through his blue hair. "No one else in my family has magic, so I've never even seen it done."

"I made some shadow pictures before. Never lasted more than a few minutes, though." I shrugged. "It will be interesting, trying to channel Umbral energy in such a bright room."

"Oh, yeah. Wow. I didn't think of that." Ian shook his head, wincing with the movement.

"I'll manage. It's about getting the theory in this class, anyway." I shrugged. "I can always make shadows around a small object with my hands."

"Yeah." Charles breathed out a sigh that probably sounded more relieved than he'd intended.

I glanced up to see Nox hurry into the room alone, looking more put together than usual, though her eyes seemed slightly vacant. It reminded me of the time I'd seen Olivia after she had her Adderal. She pulled a jet-black patch of what looked like fur from her bag and tucked it under her shirt, pressing it to her stomach. I blinked, barely able to believe my eyes as it melded with her skin, vanishing entirely. Droplets of water beaded up on her face, smelling distinctly of a dank fen or riverbank. Her hair dampened and increased in volume, taking on that unkempt appearance I'd thought was just her desired look. She dabbed her face with a small gym towel. Her eyes gleamed with an awareness they'd lacked before.

"Sorry about the swamp smell, guys." Nox's face reddened a little as she hung her head.

"Oh! I had no idea you were a Kelpie until now." Ian just barely stopped himself from clapping his hands. "I've never met a Faerie shifter before."

"It's okay. I usually keep it down on low, but that's what I get for hitting the snooze button too many times. I've been wiped all week. My magic feels sparse. Usually, Unseelie energy's all over the place this time of year. It's why I'm taking this class over the inter-session."

"Huh, what could possibly be displacing seasonal Faerie magic?" Ian chewed his bottom lip.

"Hmm." I tapped my pencil against my book. "A bunch of Seelie creatures in the area, a Magus who can siphon Fae energy, unseasonably warm weather, a Seelie artifact washing up on the beach. Stuff like that."

"Wow, you know more than I'd think about that kind of thing, Maddie." Nox peered at me from under her long, thick bangs.

"I spent most of last night studying magic creatures and energy. Some friends are taking Terminology and Creature Classification." I smiled, hoping she wouldn't ask for a list.

"Study buddy osmosis learning, huh?" Nox actually smiled.

"Something like that." I looked up at the clock, saw it was time for class to start. "Where's Professor Thurston?"

"Maybe she's getting things for us to make gadgets out of." Charles flipped over a flashcard. "Ugh, will I ever remember this coincidence postulate?"

"Which one?" Ian leaned against Charles' shoulder, picking up the card. "Oh. Coincidence Denial. That's tricky because it should really be called Coincidence Defiance."

"How so?" Nox dropped her workbook and pencils on the bench without even looking at them. She headed over to flip over the flashcard, then read off the back. "One way to attempt breaking a coincidence pattern, Coincidence Denial is the attempt to change a likely magical outcome by repeating the pattern with one or more major changes."

"That's a vague and confused way of putting it." I shook my head. "No wonder you have trouble remembering it. How about thinking of it like lucid dreaming? Instead of waking up, you stay asleep and give yourself a weapon or some friends to fight the danger."

"So, Coincidence Denial is to recognize the pattern and doing something about it that the last poor sap didn't get to try?" Charles smiled. "Except I'll think of The Dark Tower. Like when Roland had the horn at the end of the series, you know next time it'll be different for him. Thanks, Maddie. That helped me get my brain around it way better."

"You've got lucky study buddies." Nox turned her head toward the door, but not before I caught the weary look in her eyes. "I think the Professor just walked in downstairs."

"Thanks, Nox." I faked a smile. Something was bothering my lab partner. It occurred to me that maybe she'd be helpful if the summoner had Faerie creatures at his disposal. Maybe she'd even know something about that Djinn lamp. I banished the thought. She had her own issues. It'd be insensitive to just jump in asking for help without finding out if she felt up for anything besides classwork.

Nox ran her hand through her hair, giving me a better look at her eyes. They looked bloodshot and a little puffy as though she'd been about to cry. It was awfully early to be that down in the dumps. I wasn't exactly a morning person, but sleep always sort of reset my emotional state. Either Nox had bad news that morning, or she hadn't slept. I'd want to talk to her later. Just as I was thinking I should text Lynn and ask her whether a Kelpie might be helpful, Professor Thurston arrived.

"Today's activity is important but difficult. I don't expect any of you to succeed at making a permanent gadget. That said, if you can't understand the principles behind imbuing an item with your particular school, you're going to have a rough go of things this session." The Professor set a large cardboard box on the instructor's bench. It rattled, as though it contained a collection of things. "Come up and get an item to work with."

I dragged my chair back to the bench next to Nox. I waited with her, letting Charles, Ian, and then the Kelpie go up first. She rummaged in the box with her eyes closed. That told me she knew a thing or two about coincidence herself. It seemed like the sort of thing Blaine would do. I'd have to ask him about it once he'd taken his own Magic Theory class next semester.

I copied Nox, looking away instead of closing my eyes as I felt around in the box. It wouldn't get me in trouble since this wasn't a test. The item that met my hand felt long and cold with a sharp point on one end. Its texture wasn't metal, but some other rigid substance. I didn't look at whatever it was until I got back to my seat.

"Woah." Nox had looked before I did. "That's seriously creepy, Maddie." She recoiled from my hand and the object it held. "You have to give it to Professor Thurston, like now."

I looked down and saw a vampire fang attached to a chain by a jump ring. I shuddered but managed to keep from flinging it away, then got up immediately. The croissant threatened to leap out of my throat as though my body itself was trying to eject the horror of what I held. The only way a vampire fang stayed intact once pulled was if he or she was awake and aware throughout getting defanged and was killed directly afterward. Necklaces like this had been trophies during the time just after the Big Reveal, their makers prosecuted for crimes against Extrahumanity and imprisoned for life afterward. What was one of these doing in the lab box?

"Um, Professor?" I held the necklace out to her, shivering as though I stood in an arctic wind instead of a climate-controlled magic lab.

"I'm calling the Police." Professor Thurston pulled a handkerchief from her pocket, plucking the fang from my hand with it. I was struck by how pale the Professor's face got, but nothing else besides her short words indicated her alarm.

I stood in front of her bench as she took the room phone from the wall to report the grisly discovery. The Providence Police had a Magical Forensics unit. Maybe it was old, a relic of a more turbulent time. There'd still be an investigation. There was no statute of limitations on murder. Professor Thurston placed the handkerchief-wrapped fang in a warded bag and set it on her desk.

"I expect the rest of you to begin imbuing your items. Miss May, with me please." The Professor gestured to the space beside her. I walked behind the bench, waiting as she described a semi-circle over our heads with one finger. A privacy spell, Air magic. I'd had no idea which school she had until then. Now, where had I heard about someone using Air magic recently? Last night? I almost had it when the Professor spoke.

"Now that we won't be overheard, tell me when the last time you saw the fellow who made your amulet was?" She sniffed, jaw clenched. "Henry Baxter, I believe is the name on your amulet's registry slip?"

"Last night, probably around eleven. And yes, that's Henry Baxter. Memory Psychic. He's a vampire too."

"I'm well aware of Mr. Baxter's talents, his state of being, and his history." Her gaze met mine, gray-blue and airy. "He's been a positive force in Providence's Extrahuman community since the late 1970s, decades before he got turned. I went to High School with him, you know."

"Is he okay?" I asked her the only question that mattered right then though her statements raised fifty more in my mind.

"If you saw him last night, then yes." She sighed, her voice carrying a relief her posture didn't reveal. "I could tell by looking that the fang you found is nearly a week old."

"Wait, what?" I shuddered. "You mean it's not from before the Equal Rights trials?"

"Most certainly not." She glanced down at my right hand, which had held the necklace. "It's in a warded bag now, but take a look at your hand. There are residual traces, still visible. Check closely."

I did as Professor Thurston asked, turning my head so I could squint out of the corner of my eye. Then, I gasped. A trace the approximate shape of the fang hovered squarely in the middle of my palm. The magic energy was a combination of types, but unmistakable. All three types were familiar, after all.

"Death, Unliving, and Umbral, all recent." I blinked, feeling tears prick the corners of my eyes. "Umbral stuff's all mine. And something fuzzy that I can't make out."

"Psychic energy. Telepathic." I looked up to see Professor Thurston holding a monocle over her left eye. "Here. Have a quick look." She handed the device over.

I took it gingerly with my left hand, not wanting to disrupt the energies I'd be looking at. I closed my right eye, unable to make my sight multi-task the way the Professor could. Age and experience were huge advantages in that department. It's why we went to school, after all. I saw the shimmer resolve into a smoky violet hue. Telepathic Psychic energy. I couldn't figure out why that was there. Unliving energy was key to preserving pulled fangs. The Death energy came from the vampire's demise. Was I looking at the Summoner's handiwork? They had a sort of telepathy with their creatures through the anchors binding them. My mind wasn't officially blown, but it was a near thing.

Professor Thurston held out her hand. I placed the monocle

in it, blinking a little more. This time, I had to wipe the corners of my eyes. The Grim hadn't gotten Henry, but had killed someone else instead. There had to be two dead vampires by now. The summoner was killing on campus, but why?

"Is there something you want to tell me, Miss May?" Professor Thurston pursed her lips, expectant instead of puzzled. "It's an interesting coincidence that fang went to your hand. There's a reason for it."

"Yes." I couldn't tell her the details of the first Grim attack. Only two people could, and only one would matter. "You need to talk to Henry Baxter as soon as possible. A Grim attacked him at the Nocturnal Lounge the night before inter-session started, and again last night at the library."

"Grims can't preserve fangs, Miss May." She drummed her fingers on the benchtop. "The police will not believe a vampire, not even one as upstanding as Henry Baxter. They will require nothing less than hard evidence."

"I know." I looked up, locking gazes with her. "But it happened. The Grim's Summoner could have preserved the fang. I have no idea who'd be able to control one, though. Definitely not a student, not even at the graduate level. Summoning is Doctoral work, according to all the PPC guidelines, right, Professor?"

"Astute observations, Miss May, but they don't explain the Telepathic energy being on the fang." Professor Thurston raised an eyebrow as her watch beeped. She held my gaze but tilted her head at the box of items. "I truly appreciate the extra knowledge and life experience non-traditional students bring to the college experience. For now, please take another item and do the activity. I've got more calls to make."

She snapped her fingers, and the privacy spell popped like a bubble. She walked to the door, heels clicking hollowly against the white floor. I reached into the box again, looking down as soon as I withdrew my hand this time. The circular object in my hand was a medallion stamped with a wolf on one side and a set of fangs on the other. The chain it dangled from was old, definitely from before the Big Reveal. It was an old alliance medallion, the kind that bound a vampire to a wolf shifter pack.

Now, what kind of coincidence could that tie me to? I pushed the question away for the time being. I had a lab to pass after all.

CHAPTER ELEVEN

Henry

I'd been sleeping when the phone rang. Yes, vampires can sleep even if most don't. It conserves blood, letting us feed less. I'd wanted an actual break while PPC was mostly closed, but recent events meant I'd spent as much time out as during the Fall semester. I was the school's oldest freshman, so I had my habits. Supposedly I'd liked them, but I jumped when that phone rang. It could be Maddie. I woke up smiling at the thought.

I shook off the emotion along with any trace of drowsiness. Last night, I'd made that promise to step back. It didn't matter that I'd been happier with her around. Friends could make each other happy from a nice, safe distance. She deserved a chance to meet someone who wasn't a second-class citizen, to have more than one choice.

"Hello?" I picked up my dumb phone. I preferred that to the smartphone in my apartment.

"Henry, I've just been told you were attacked by a Grim.

Twice. And you didn't bother notifying me." I'd know that voice if I unlived a thousand years. Henrietta, my old friend from High School. Also, the stopping point for any buck passed around PPC.

"Yes, Headmistress Thurston." I figured that was the way you greeted an old friend who'd abruptly stopped speaking to you decades earlier.

"Don't you dare Headmistress or Professor me, Henry Baxter." Her voice came through in a whispery yet still strident tone. "This is life-or-death business, and you didn't tell me. Why?"

"Didn't want you stuck with that kind of mess again. Or have you forgotten the last time that happened?" She knew I meant the hostage situation that had ended in Dahlia's death and my turning. The Extrahuman authorities hadn't believed her then, even with her new husband's sterling reputation and deep connections.

"I haven't." Her voice didn't exactly soften, but the edges blunted at least. "This is different. One of my Magic Theory students pulled a fang out of the amulet box."

"Please don't tell me it was Maddie May who found that terrible thing." I held a breath I didn't need. "She's a good egg, shouldn't get involved in something like this."

"Too bad. She already did. Like most Umbral magi, Miss May's got a sleuthing streak a mile wide." Henrietta sighed. "I know you two are acquainted."

"Not so much. I just made her the amulet that lets her go to this class of yours." I scratched my head. "By the way, doesn't some Russian guy usually teach Magic Theory?"

"Don't lie. You spent more time with her than that." I could picture the face she'd be making to go with those words—a coy little lopsided grin. Henrietta had always smiled more with the left side of her face than the right.

"Fine. I've seen her off-campus twice. The rest of the time was just studying in a group." I tapped one finger against my nightstand. "Don't avoid the question about that Professor you're replacing, though. I've got one of my hunches."

"Fine back, then. Hold on." I heard shoes clicking on tile and a faint echo as Henrietta moved away from what or whoever she'd been standing near before. The faint squeak of a hinge told me she'd gone through a door. "He took an emergency leave two days before classes began. Didn't give a reason except to say he had to take care of some sleep issues he's been having."

"And this is Professor Brodsky, right? The double Ph.D. who also runs the Summoning research lab?"

"I'll send someone from Campus Police down to look in on him." A faint scrape and clink sounded, then Henrietta took a deep breath. "Since he's on medical leave, they won't even raise an eyebrow about that sort of thing." Her exhale was unmistakable.

"Hey, you should re-quit with the smoky treats. Those things'll kill you."

"You try integrating and running a school where your star pupils get walloped by a snowstorm one session and two buildings get trashed by a Grim the next." I heard her take another drag. "You'd get back on whatever your worst habit was, too."

"Insane amounts of coffee milk isn't as fatal as the cancer sticks. It's also not the same on the palate as it used to be." I surprised myself with a little snicker. "Quit them."

"Why don't we talk like this more often, Henry?" She'd turned a faucet on to cover her laughter. She had to be in the restroom.

"Because you're Professor Henrietta Thurston, former Prom Queen and Headmistress of the only Ivy League school for Extrahumans in the United States." I leaned back against the wall behind my bed. "I'm just a two-bit Psychic who happened to be friends with her crew, then went and got one of them killed and himself turned."

"Quit with the self-deprecation, Baxter." Her voice was still thready and breathless after all the giggling, but her tone had gone back from High School reminiscent to serious business in a second flat. "You risked your neck to stop that Extramagus. You'd have died just like poor Dahlia if the vampire you rescued hadn't had enough energy to turn you."

"Maybe, maybe not." I stared up at the bare wall on the other side of my one-room apartment. "But I wasn't forgettable like she was."

"That whole event's right there in the texts we assign for Local Extrahuman History, I'll have you know."

"Too bad they don't name the Extramagus or the vamps along with the champs in any of those books."

"Sometimes, a curse is a blessing, Henry. At least that's what Rick used to say." I heard the unmistakable muffled squeak of gritted teeth. Smoking wasn't the only bad habit she'd reverted to, then.

"I'm surprised you brought him up." Rick was her ex-husband, former Prom King and Dean of Students before PPC got integrated. He'd tolerated me while I was still really alive because Henrietta loved her friends, but was the main reason everyone besides Dahlia's boyfriend Neil had cut me off after I got vamped. I thought I remembered him believing us about the Extramagus though. "I was really surprised you two didn't last, all things considered."

"Well, sometimes you have to choose between your home life and your job." Henrietta sighed again. "No. That's not true. I just couldn't do it anymore. Put up with his bigotry. It got worse after I integrated the school." I'd thought she shunned me because of Dahlia's death. That would be easier to take than her giving in to her husband's bigotry. "Sorry, I didn't intend on saying anything about all that."

"Look, you should talk to someone about it, maybe more frequently if you already do." I couldn't imagine she didn't have a therapist. "But I'm not remotely the best person to be your sounding board."

"For what it's worth, I'm sorry."

"For what it's worth, I'm not." I pushed my feet into the slippers I kept at the edge of my bed. "Keeping a low profile once I got back probably saved my life. It would have been dangerous getting involved with Rick's brand of Extrahuman politicking. Anyway, I bet Maddie already told you to look around the Lounge and the tunnels by Water Place Park."

"She did. But if that fang turned up in the box today, we probably won't find anything until whoever's doing this gets caught."

"Or until it happens again."

"Yes, that." I heard her turn the tap off. "Maybe whoever Campus Police sends will find a clue at Professor Brodsky's apartment."

"We can hope." I shuffled into the kitchen to warm up some water for tea. I still hadn't been out to get more coffee.

"Call if you discover anything else." I heard the hinge squeak again, and the echo of her footsteps in the hall. "Goodbye, Mr. Baxter."

"Bye." My old-fashioned flip phone let me hang up before she did. There are no small victories, just small victors.

I filled and plugged in the electric kettle. My apartment just had a refrigerator, counters, and cabinets. Technically it wouldn't be legal to rent a place without a stove to anyone living, but for me it was fine. The last thing I wanted was a gas fire caused by an appliance I didn't even use. I got the tea tin down from the cabinet above the microwave. Someone came in through the door upstairs, into the hall. I scooped loose tea into the infuser over my favorite mug, then froze at footsteps on my basement stairs. What kind of unhinged person would visit a vampire before noon?

The knock on my door was light and unexpected. I'd just braced myself for property destruction and a fight-or-flight situation. Then, I breathed in deeply through my nose. Of course. Lynn had given Olivia an errand for today. No one mentioned it'd have anything to do with me, but I caught the dry feathery scent of owl shifter outside. I knew it wasn't some other bird shifter because she was the only one taking an Adderal and Ritalin cocktail every day. Those had a distinctive smell, too.

I unlocked the knob, the bolts, and the chain. When I opened the door, I caught Olivia in mid-yawn.

"Sorry." She blinked. "For yawning in your face and bothering you at this ungodly hour."

"If it's ungodly, why aren't you sleeping?" I gave her a sideways glance, waving her in. "Tony's nocturnal too, and he sleeps until at least two in the afternoon every day." I pulled out one of the chairs at the small table doubling as a kitchenette and room divider. Such is life in studio apartments.

"Tony's lucky. Lynn sent me on a mission today. Our Terminology class just has a test on Fridays, so once I finished, I went all over campus." Olivia pulled a series of paper bags from the big brown satchel she always carried. "I found some things. Only touched them with gloves on. Lynn wants to see if you can get anything from them." She shuddered even though I kept my apartment ten-ish degrees above what keeps pipes from freezing. Her eyes were wider than usual.

"What's wrong?" I glanced down at the brown paper bags on the table.

"You're not going to like some of this stuff." Olivia yawned again, looking like she'd rather be anywhere but here.

"There are tons of things I don't like. I won't freak out or anything, but if you want to, you can leave." I nodded at the unlocked door. The fact that I hadn't redone even one of the bolts pricked at my mind like a waking limb.

"I'm not supposed to until you're done. I have to bring them back so Blaine can do his dragon thing with them tomorrow."

"Okay, then." I got up to shut off the boiling kettle. "You want some tea?" I glanced at the door instead of Olivia. I was a lousy host.

"Tea?! Definitely." She got a hungry look on her face that I'd begun to associate with Bobby Tremain in the dining hall. I pottered around the kitchen, rummaging at the back of the cabinet for sugar and non-dairy creamer. I never used it myself, but my landlord did. The tea always went on when he came to collect the rent.

Just as I'd finished setting her infuser up, I heard the snick of the lower deadbolt. Owl shifters were perceptive, but I hadn't expected one living diurnally to have much awareness. She'd noticed my discomfort. Maybe that said more about me than Olivia. All the recent socialization had shaken something loose. It'd take a while to settle down and fortify the armor I usually wore against the world.

The tea steeped as I brought the sugar and creamer to the table with some spoons. I set out saucers and napkins, avoiding the ominous bags for as long as I could. When I turned back with the mugs, Olivia headed back toward the table after taking a detour past my bookshelf. Owl shifters loved books like dragon shifters loved their hoards.

"So, what do you think?" I watched her pull the infuser out of the mug and set it on the saucer.

"Not enough High Fantasy, too much proto-horror. I'm not a Lovecraft fan, but Poe is nice." Olivia sprinkled sugar in her tea, then heaped two teaspoons of powdered ersatz cream in after it. "You ought to try Robert Howard."

"I have. An absent friend swore by his work, but it just never caught on up here." I pointed at my temple, then took the infuser out of my own tea, inhaling deeply. Black, like my vampiric existence. The thought made me smile just a little.

"Do you have a lot of those?" Olivia gazed down at the light tan tea thoughtfully. "Absent friends, I mean."

"More than I'd like."

"Listen, one of the things you're not going to like is from the Nocturnal Lounge. Fred Redford found it."

"I figured." I took another sip. "What about the rest of them?"

"One's from the library."

"How did you get in there?"

"Work-study. I digitize stuff in the media lab. I told them I had to get some homework, and they let me in." She tasted her tea, made a face, added more sugar. "I found an amulet. Round brass thing, the size of a pocket watch."

"Wait, what?" It was my turn to blink like a sleepy owl.

"I shouldn't tell you more. Lynn said your impressions should be as unbiased as possible." She tried the tea again and nodded at it this time. "Maybe I already said too much."

"No, it's okay. I'll do a mind-clearing exercise before I start." I inhaled the scent of bergamot again, bracing myself before starting. "Glad they're separated. I won't know what I'm getting with my eyes."

"Exactly what Lynn said."

"It's comforting when a super-genius agrees with you." I set the paper bags in a line, then reached out to pull one closer, opened it, and stuck my hand inside.

The object in my hand was instantly familiar. I remembered working on that amulet for the better part of three months, making mistakes and having to undo my impressions several times. Even the ribbon it hung from felt like an old friend. The energy coming off it was distinctly psychic but bonded to magic. Umbral magic, because no one else would need an amulet like this. Thing is, there weren't any other Umbral magi at PPC, or even registered in Providence. I shook my head. The magic on the amulet held a feel of age and experience.

"This is an amulet I made for suppressing Umbral magic." I took my hand out of the bag, leaving it inside. "But I don't remember who it was for."

"Is there a way to check that?"

"Maybe, maybe not. Depends on whether I made it before or after the Big Reveal. There'd be a registry slip if it was after. I might have stored the memory of binding it in an item, but that's somewhere I can't get to until Monday." Olivia didn't need to know I kept a collection of trinkets in a safe-deposit box at the Providence Underground Bank.

"Well, you got some information to start with, anyway." Olivia leaned back and sipped more tea.

I shrugged and grabbed the bag in the middle. At first, I thought nothing was in there, but my fingertips brushed something warm and diaphanous. I closed my eyes, trying to get my hand around whatever it was. A thin and delicate netting wriggled against my palm, its warmth less unsettling than its stickiness. It clung, wrapping itself firmly around my fingers, binding them together. It could only be one thing.

"Spider shifter silk?"

"Crazy, huh?" I couldn't see Olivia, but she was smart. She'd be leaning away from the table. No one wanted to tangle with this stuff, literally. It'd let me go since I wasn't technically alive. "That's what Fred found in the rubble of your table, by the way."

"And he gave it to you?" I opened my eyes, all done with my impressions.

"Well, he made me bring Bobby." Olivia shrugged. "Wouldn't give it to me directly. Thinks I'm untrustworthy because I stay up all day."

"Ah. Everybody loves the all-American bear shifter." I waited for the silk to uncoil and settle back inside the bag, then folded the top over probably more than I had to. "Even Changelings likely to tithe Unseelie."

"Fred hasn't taken his mantle yet?" Olivia blinked. "I wonder why."

"No idea. Maybe ask Tony." I leaned my elbows on the table.

"Um, no rush on that." Olivia's cheeks pinked. "Anyway, what did you get?"

"It wasn't put there by a spider shifter. It's a spy device. Like a magical nanny cam."

"So that means checking the registry's not going to help us?"

"Probably not. You can get spider shifter silk in half the magic supply shops in Rhode Island." I wiggled my fingers, then paused to take another slug of my tea. "Mainly, this just tells us we're not looking for a spider shifter. Would a shady Extramagus or his Psychic friends register spyware?"

"No way. So what are we looking for?"

"Magi or Psychics who can make that kind of device and are connected to PPC." I took a few calming breaths as I gazed at the last remaining bag. I had a hinky feeling about it. "Might want to start with Professor Brodsky, who went on medical leave just before inter-session started. He's a Summoner, you know. They're Psychic."

"Okay." Olivia jotted a few things down on a small notepad, then held her tea in both hands between herself and the last bag. I didn't blame her.

"Well, here goes nothing."

As I extended my hand, the clock across the square from my building struck twelve and my phone rang again. I grabbed that instead of the bag. That had to be a sign.

"Hello?" The connection sounded like the caller was outside in the wind.

"Henry."

"Maddie." I cleared my throat. "What's up?"

"Are you okay? You sound like you got a stay of execution." She seemed to just get me, but then again she might just get vibes. Having two psychic parents does that to people.

"It's been a hectic morning." I held one finger up, signaling to Olivia that I might be on the phone a while. She smiled, curling her hands around her mug.

"I know. Professor Thurston called you." The connection cleared like she'd gotten out of the wind.

"That was a cakewalk compared to the errand Lynn has Olivia on." I grimaced at the bag, then shrugged at Olivia. "Memory psychometry isn't anyone's idea of fun."

"Ouch."

"None of that's the reason you called." I hoped she didn't call just to hear my voice even though I was way too glad to hear hers.

"Yeah, um, I guess." The hemming and hawing didn't bode well for putting distance between us. "Look, the fang had Telepathic energy on it. I can't figure out why. Does that fit with Summoners? I know they get something like it with their creature contracts. But on a fang, it doesn't make sense."

"Not that I've ever heard of, unless Mind magic's involved. Why not talk to Lynn about it, or Blaine?"

"Yeah, I guess I should." I could hear the smile in her voice. "Thanks, Henry. Sorry for bothering you while you were busy."

"Don't be sorry. Psychometry's like a grab bag full of broken glass and venomous snakes. I'm glad to get any kind of break from it. Bye, Maddie."

"Bye." I kept the phone open until she hung up. After that, I put the device down and set my head in my hands.

"You've got it bad." Olivia's voice made me sit up. I'd almost forgotten she was there. Her face wore a slight but wistful grin, her eyes dripped with empathy.

"Um, what?" I shouldn't have let Olivia see that.

"Never mind." She glanced at the most awful brown paper bag in the entire city of Providence and shuddered a bit. "Might as well get it over with, right?"

I groaned like I used to the morning after a night at the clubs. At least hangovers didn't happen to vampires. I reached for the bag again. I got a tingle just from putting my hand inside. Whatever was in there had a familiar feel to it. I couldn't help myself, I trembled a little.

Once I held the wider-than-average card, I knew exactly what it was, where it had been found, and why it was here. I gulped, a reflex left over from my mortal days. An image came up behind my tightly closed eyes, one that should have been heartwarming but gave me a deep chill instead. I dropped the card back in the bag and closed it, understanding I'd get nothing else from it. Blaine probably would. I'd want to know exactly what he got off it right away, too.

"That's Headmistress Thurston's. It's The Lovers, a tarot card her ex-husband gave her on their wedding day." I shuddered. "Trouble is, the emotion in there is all wrong for her. It smacks of regret and missing someone, but I know that's absolutely not true."

"So why'd I find it at what Providence Police are now calling a murder scene?" Olivia turned her head and looked at me out of the corner of her eye.

"Someone's trying to frame her for a hate crime." I explained about the vampire fang in the lab box. "And if I'd been the victim, it'd make perfect sense."

"Who'd want to do a thing like that?" She blinked slowly a few times. "And who'd believe it?"

"Her best friend got killed rescuing a vampire. You're an Extrahuman Law student. You know any detective worth his salt would pin that motive on her." I took a deep breath, but it fell far short of calming. "There's nothing more I can tell you until Blaine has a go at it." I pushed the bags across the table toward her. "I have to be there when Blaine does his thing. We'll need to talk."

"Blaine wants to do it alone." She plucked the bags from the table, then stowed them in her satchel.

"Tough." I crossed my arms.

"He'll be a dragon. Scaly. Massive. Big teeth." Olivia fastened the clasp on her bag and got up, heading toward the door.

"Nothing I haven't seen." I rolled my eyes, leaning back in my chair.

"He's a fire dragon." Her eyebrows tried to make friends with her hairline as she undid the deadbolt.

"Okay, scary. I'll manage." I uncrossed my arms and shrugged. "You tell them."

"I will." She turned the knob and pushed the door open, standing in it for a moment. "Owl shifters always leave pellets of wisdom for their hosts. Here's yours. The best-laid plans of Magi and monsters often go awry."

"What's that supposed to mean?" I stood up, collecting the tea things.

"I think part of you knows already. Bye, Henry. Thanks for the tea." She shut the door behind her. I bolted it before finishing clearing up.

CHAPTER TWELVE

Maddie

I pushed through the door at street level, finally done with class. I'd imbued the charm with Umbral energy that still hadn't worn off. No one's had. Our homework was to record how long the energy lasted and one more attempt over the weekend. Nox hurried out the door with me. I stopped short, and we collided. I ended up on all fours with scraped palms. Nox tripped right over me, stumbling headlong into Josh Dennison.

They were a tangle of limbs at the bottom of the steps. Muffled exclamations of surprise and annoyance had me stifling laughter as I stood up and brushed myself off. They looked like a giant amalgamated spider. I reached a hand down and grabbed one of Nox's. It was cold and a bit clammy, exactly what I'd expect from a Kelpie.

Josh's eyes followed our movement as I helped her up. Her breath plumed out white in the cold air, carrying a stammer of laughter along with it. I held my hand out to help Josh up, but he shook his head and rose on his own. I also laughed. Couldn't help it.

"Great Goblin's Garters, that's hilarious!" Nox held her shaking sides with one hand and pointed at Josh's chest with the other.

"I know, right?" I leaned on a lamp post to steady myself, gasping words out between giggles.

"What's so funny?" Josh put his hands on his hips, feet shoulder's width apart. His face wore the most menacing frown he could probably manage. Other people might be scared of an angry wolf shifter, but it didn't faze either of us. After all, Nox could turn into a magical Unseelie horse, and I could hide if Josh wolfed out.

"Didn't look before you put your shirt on today, huh?" I pressed a hand to my breastbone, trying to suppress the giggle fit.

"Leaping Luna, I did it again?" He pulled down the hem of his t-shirt, peering at it. I watched his lips form the words "Fuck you, you fucking fuck." He rolled his eyes, reminding me of Lynn on an extra-sarcastic day.

"Yup." I shook my head. "You wore the rudest shirt in the known universe again."

"Wait, again?" Nox's question came complete with a curious glimmer in her eye. "You mean he's worn that in public before?"

"Yeah, I did. That was the worst presentation grade I ever got." Josh sighed. "I'll have to do something about that before I go on my Campus Police business."

"And how." I blinked. "Wait. You have Campus Police business?"

"Yeah. Gotta check on some professor on emergency medical leave. No one's heard from him and the Headmistress is worried."

"Hmm." I wanted to tell Josh more, but probably shouldn't in front of Nox. She didn't know about the Grim problem.

"Oh, wow." Nox put one hand over her mouth. "The only Professor on leave is Brodsky, the guy who was supposed to teach Magic Theory. Can I go with you? I had him last semester and actually liked him."

My voice mingled with Josh's as we spoke simultaneously. "Sure, let's all go—" "Um, that's not a good idea—" We stopped, glaring at each other.

"Look, I have to go change my shirt before heading over to Brodsky's anyway." Josh still held my gaze like the Alpha heir he was, but it softened a bit. "Why don't we all go and Maddie can tell me what her issue is with having company on a mission like this."

"Okay." I re-settled my satchel on my shoulder.

Nox just nodded and hitched her backpack up her arms. We followed Josh along Hope Street, heading toward Swan Point Cemetery. He took a left toward the hoity-toity houses between Hope and the Blackstone Valley Parkway. Those were multi-million dollar properties. I hadn't imagined someone like Josh living here. No wonder he didn't have a room on campus. Then again, his dad headed PPC Campus Police, and his mom was the Extrahuman liaison to the Rhode Island State Police. Of course, they lived in an exclusive area. This was Rhode Island, and any position of power came with benefits. And I thought Blaine was the only rich kid I knew.

Nox's eyes practically bugged out of her head when Josh stopped at a wrought-iron gate. Her power came from an Unseelie Faerie object. No wonder that gate freaked her out. It had spikes in front and on top, definitely the fashion at the turn of the twentieth century. Nox swallowed audibly, gripping the straps of her backpack so tightly her knuckles blanched.

"Sorry about the gate." Josh grinned more gently at Nox than I expected. "We'd take it down, but we're on the Register of Historic Places. They won't let us without a ton of red tape." I felt my eyebrows knit together, wondering why Josh would fib about something like that. Umbral Affinity sometimes let me know when people hid the truth. He must have told her a whopper.

"It's okay. I'll be fine in a sec." Nox set her backpack on the ground at her feet. She unzipped it and pulled a small oilcloth pouch from inside. Then, she put her right hand under her shirt and murmured words in a language I couldn't recognize.

Josh blinked as she pulled a slick black rectangle of pelt from under her shirt. She tucked it into the oilcloth pouch, a few drops of swampy-smelling water dripping to the sidewalk in the process. After that, she put the pouch back in her pack and zipped it. I'd seen the difference the pelt made in her appearance that morning. What really struck me was the change in her attitude.

Nox's lips pulled back in an easy smile as she put her backpack back on. Her hair lost its wet and bedraggled look, and when she tucked it behind her ears, it stayed put. Her eyes were blue-green, something I hadn't noticed before. As she walked through the now open gate, her stride was long but more tentative, with a hint of feminine sway she'd lacked before.

"You two have your talk." Nox glanced over her shoulder at us as she ambled ahead up the long tree-lined driveway. "I'll meet you halfway up."

"Well, that was unexpected." Josh turned around to close the gate behind us. "She's something else. How long have you known her?"

"Just since the first day of class." I grinned at Josh. "And that's part of the problem."

"Oh?" He walked slowly toward the house.

"Yeah." I followed. "This Brodsky thing's more than what it seems. I was with Professor Thurston when she called Campus Police. She thinks he knows something about the Grim."

"He's the Summoning Professor. That's not a huge mental leap to make."

"I know. I think she suspects him, but needs hard evidence."

"So this might be more dangerous than checking to see if the old guy had a coronary. And we shouldn't bring a Kelpie as powerful as Nox seems to be. Why?"

"Because she doesn't know about all this. I believe Blaine's tinfoil hat theory, that there's an Extramagus messing with the school. Nox shouldn't get mixed up in that unwittingly."

"I get it." Josh shrugged. "But not everyone reacts the same when the going gets tough. If she's like me, she will welcome a distraction. But Brodsky can't call the Grim again for five more days."

"Who knows what else he could call up, though."

"Gotta check his apartment to find out. If he's there, he'll cooperate, wouldn't want to blow his cover by messing with us. If not, we might find Thurston's evidence." Josh shook his head. "Look, I'm not a brain like Lynn or a Boy Scout like Bobby. I'm dangerous in a fight, but that's not all there is to being a wolf shifter. I know how to play a mission like this. Both Mom and Dad are Alphas. I cut my teeth on double-speak. But I don't know Faeries. Bet you dollars to donuts Nox does."

"Okay, fine. I still have a weird feeling about bringing her in on this, but I'll let you decide. It's bad enough Lynn got Olivia involved. She's half-asleep all the time."

"Why an owl shifter wants to be diurnal is beyond me." He shook his head. "Crazy bird."

"True story."

"Leaping Luna, you sound like Baxter." He shook his head, then walked along in silence briefly. "You should spend time with someone else for a change."

"Huh?"

"Come out with me tomorrow night." Josh turned to face me, walking backward when side-stepped and continued up the driveway.

"Um." I chewed on my lower lip. I wasn't sure about how Josh looked at me. It wasn't romantic or lusty, just protective. Definitely not the way a girl wants to get asked out. "Where?"

"Dunno. Wherever." He stopped at the circular part of the drive, near the huge house's entrance. Nox stood with her back to us, gazing at the intricate woodwork on the top of the gabled roof.

"Hey, Nox, want to come out with us tomorrow night?"

"Sure!" She looked over her shoulder just as Josh turned. And there was the spark that had been missing from Josh's face before. He said nothing, turning his head away from her before she could look him in the face. I was struck by how controlled he was. If that was the life of a wolf shifter Alpha, I felt more than a little sorry for him. Nox and I waited while Josh went inside.

"I didn't expect this much of a difference." I glanced at Nox's backpack. "It seems like there shouldn't be one at all."

"That's because our skins carry more than magic and shifting ability." Nox scuffed the pale gravel coating the driveway with the toe of one boot. "They have ancestry in them, too. Little quirks and personality traits from generations back, compliments of all my forebears who wore it. The more ancestors, the stronger the magic."

"Wow. Is it distracting?"

"Sometimes. It's not like I hear most of them all the time, they just affect my mood. That and my appearance." She smirked, then gestured at her torso. "I'm the first woman in my family to inherit it after twelve generations. My grandpa's not happy that number thirteen's a girl. His influence in there is the hardest part. He fights me on anything too feminine."

"And I thought my life being forgotten by half of everyone sucks." I realized that if she'd inherited it, she must have lost her father already.

"Guess I'm still getting used to it. The magic's a huge benefit." She smiled, but not with her eyes. "I was mundane before, so I love that part. I took to Water magic like a duck."

We laughed together easily, a heartrending change in light of that morning's horror. I still thought Nox shouldn't get involved countering the person trying to wreck PPC. I thought about coincidence. Maybe involving Nox wasn't up to me. I'd call my mother tomorrow, ask her about the future.

Josh came out of the door, wearing a navy-blue Campus Police shirt. He smiled, but the expression didn't really touch his eyes until he glanced at Nox. That was another puzzle. Why ask me on a date when he was clearly more interested in the Kelpie? For some reason, I thought it'd be a bad idea to call him on the carpet right here and now.

The walk down the drive was quicker than the one up. We headed across Hope Street and down the hill on Rochambeau, then turned up a narrow driveway. We stood at the side door of a yellow sided triple-decker. Josh rang the bell for number three, the one with Brodsky's name beside it. He waited, then rang again. No response. Then, he pressed the button for number one next to the name Kazynski. A voice came over the intercom.

"*Preevyet?*" The Russian greeting crackled with age and intercom static.

"Hi there. I'm from Providence Paranormal College, just here to check on Professor Brodsky upstairs."

"Oh, go on in." The words carried through on a heavily accented voice. "He not home, but you leave the note or something for him, *da?*"

"That's right. Thanks." Josh grabbed the doorknob just after it buzzed.

The narrow stairwell smelled strongly of wood polish. The door marked number one was on the left. A violin-shaped welcome mat sat in front of it, reminding me of a guard dog. We went up creaky stairs with low-pile carpet cushions on the risers. At the top, the door to number three stood open just a crack.

"Huh, odd." Josh made a gesture from his forehead down to his chin. I had no idea what that meant, but Nox seemed to.

"Hide us," she whispered.

I gathered shadows around us. Josh blinked, then gave a smirk and pointed at his stomach. Nox pulled her Kelpie skin out of the oilcloth pouch and tucked it under her shirt. The change was weird even after her explanation. After that, Josh turned toward the door, beckoning for us to follow as he pushed it open and went inside.

Brodsky's apartment was dim, the only light coming through drawn shades and the door behind us. It was nearly silent, too. I almost jumped out of my skin when the refrigerator compressor came to life. Nox put a hand on my arm, calming me instantly like I was relaxing in a warm bath. No wonder she liked Water magic if that's what it was like.

"Professor Brodsky?" Josh stood next to a combination coat and umbrella stand. A hat, coat, and long, black umbrella occupied half of it. "PPC Faculty sent me to see if there's anything you need." Josh glanced around, then leaned toward the hat on the rack. He closed his mouth, taking a long, deep breath through his nose. He'd be able to track Professor Brodsky if he got a recent enough scent, but he shook his head and ventured further into the apartment. We followed.

The living room had a sagging vintage couch in the middle. A crooked bundle of something brown and stick-like lay across it. I couldn't figure out what it was until it moved. It was a Brownie, a Pure Faerie. They didn't mingle with humans or reproduce by making changeling offspring. They were dangerous to talk to. If you asked them too many questions, they'd rope you into a contract just by answering. It was part and parcel with their inability to lie. A direct question counted as a contract. I hoped Josh understood that Seelie didn't mean benevolent.

"Why does the scion of the Sons of Dennis smell like, Unseelie scum?" The Brownie sat up, blinking eyes that looked like knot-holes. "Does he want to anger his parents?"

"I'm not angering anyone, wood-child." Josh put his hands out, palms up. "It comes with going to college."

"Yes, they let anyone in now. Not like the good days." The

Brownie's voice was like twigs cracking underfoot. "Don't you wish things hadn't changed, wolf-child?"

"Days are days. We live how we have to." Josh stared at the creature, unblinking. "I'd tell you to stay in the Under if you don't like it, but you're in a Summoner's house."

"Yes. His dreams are troubled and his night hours restless. Are you here to interfere with him?"

"What he does in his sleep is no concern to me."

"Perhaps it should be. I smell the unliving on you, too. Another reminder of the old days." The Brownie stood, stretching to its full and spindly height. It looked like a bunch of extra-long bamboo come to life, like the Sawhorse in L. Frank Baum's Oz books, except vertical. "Are you turning back to the old ways, courting an alliance with a vampire?"

"Just going to college, like I said." Josh chuffed out a breath. "Vampires are more trouble than they're worth." Josh's grin matched the condescending tone he cast at the Brownie. I understood the kind of bait he used here, but wasn't sure it'd work. The Brownie hissed, its limbs crackling. "Surely your host has better control of himself than a vampire."

"You're wrong, Son of Dennis. Control, yes. Of the self, no. Don't you want to know what I mean?"

"Of course, but I'll never ask while a Summoner binds you." Josh's smile was as cold and distant as a crescent moon. "That just means he gets to control what you do with my contract."

"You think you're wise." The Brownie's posture became more rigid, a sign of relaxation for their kind. "But you err. It would be a Magus who'd own any contract we make this day."

Time seemed to slow down as I watched Josh's eyebrows raise quizzically. Just as he opened his mouth, Nox surged forward, breaking free of my hiding spell. She slapped him hard across the face before he could speak.

"How dare you?!" She glowered at him with such a show of anguish and raw pain that I almost dropped my shadows.

"I'm sorry. I don't know what I did wrong." Josh looked as surprised as I felt, eyebrows like apostrophes accenting his wide eyes.

"We had a deal, and you go slumming it with a Summoner-bound Brownie?" She tapped one booted toe heavily on the hardwood floor, making a hollow, dead, wooden sound. "Don't let the creature's flattery go to your head. But with a target that big, how could it miss?"

The Brownie clattered and rustled and snapped in its unique expression of distress. It backed away, tumbling over the couch to land behind it. I heard a wooden skitter as it rushed to escape the confrontation. A hint of movement only I could see in one dark corner of the room told me it'd gone to ground. Brownies were earth-aligned Faeries. Water magic wielded by an Unseelie creature was the only thing that could banish them from this realm for a year and a day. If that happened to this one, it'd breach Brodsky's contract. The Sidhe Queen would punish the Brownie harshly. It'd do anything to avoid such a fate.

"Is that enough information to satisfy our contract, Kelpie?" Josh stared Nox right in the eye, his upper lip curling in a snarl. His fists clenched in rage. He wasn't faking any of it. Her insult had stung more than the slap. I wondered whether she knew.

"Not yet. You look around and find anything you can. I'll keep this sorry excuse for a chip off your shoulder." Nox turned to face the corner, hand outstretched in the Brownie's direction.

"Fine." Josh strode toward the small hall leading to the bath and bedrooms. I followed him, knowing the Brownie wouldn't notice Umbral magic while Nox stood over it.

In the hall, he paused, then took the left door into a bathroom with a shower stall. A single shelf held towels, soap, and anti-dandruff shampoo. The medicine cabinet contained Tylenol, a toothbrush, and a series of sleep-aids. These ranged in strength from over-the-counter to prescriptions that got heavier the further forward in time the dates got. Whatever trouble Brodsky had with sleep started in midsummer.

Josh picked up the most recent bottle, dated December 1st. He shook it, holding it up to the light. It was half-full. Professor Brodsky had stopped using pharmacological sleep methods after exams. I made a mental note to add that to the tinfoil hat notebook.

I had to step into the shower to let Josh out of the bathroom, then followed him across the hall, into an office. A shelf of textbooks and lab manuals lined one wall, all from classes Brodsky taught. Nothing out of the ordinary there. The desk had a paperweight with Umbral energy inside it. I'd recognize that anywhere, of course. Something about it was familiar. It shimmered like my amulet, an item crafted to let Psychics use magic or let Magi be Psychic. It might connect to the Grim, but its energy was faint. I pulled out my phone to tell Josh to check the paperweight.

Josh moved along to Brodsky's bedroom before he got the text. He tapped his phone, then hit Send. He'd check it after the bedroom. Josh had already taken off his jacket and shirt before I realized what he was doing. He was going to scent everything in wolf form. I looked away to give him privacy. When I heard the click of wolf paws on hardwood, I turned around.

Josh sniffed everything he could reach, which was most of it. He was rangy as a wolf which made him about my height on his hind legs. After he checked the bedroom, Josh went back to the office. I watched him sniff the paperweight, then flinch away in a backward half-jump. I stayed in the office as he checked the bathroom then went back to the bedroom. When he appeared in the hallway on two legs and fully dressed, I followed him back to the living room.

Nox hadn't moved from the spot she'd taken up earlier. Even her arm was in the same position. Just as I was about to check for magical influence, she lowered it.

"Don't ask the twig any stupid questions, wolf." She strode to the front door and stood by the hat rack. "Say bye-bye and get out of here. Once you answer my questions, our deal is done."

Josh turned to face the Brownie's corner. They crept out of the shadow, creaking and crackling as they crawled to the couch. The Brownie reminded me of a stick bug. Once stretched out across the threadbare cushions, they looked up at Josh again.

"Until we meet next, Son of Dennis." They quivered like a bird's nest in a strong breeze.

"Yes. Hopefully, under very different circumstances." He grinned.

"Indeed, we shall. And the Kelpie, too." It stiffened.

What could the Brownie mean? I wracked my brain, then remembered that Brownies had the Faerie version of Precognition. Mom always said they knew which way the winds of fate blew.

I kept to the shadows until we got back to campus, which was better than getting in the middle of the weird tension between Josh and Nox. We made plans to meet down at The Coffee Exchange on Wickenden the next night. Josh spoke with a stiff formality that hung on him like a necktie, or maybe a noose.

I wasn't going out with him alone. Nox might not come after the spat in Brodsky's apartment, but that made no difference. I sent texts to the rest of the tinfoil hat crew, then went back to my room to check my homework. The Umbral magic in the alliance medallion faded as the moon rose. I recorded it in my workbook, wondering whether I'd have time to repeat the imbuing exercise over the weekend. At least Professor Thurston would have to accept my excuses if I couldn't.

CHAPTER THIRTEEN

Henry

India Point Park was cold on Saturday, but I didn't care. I had to do something besides think about Maddie and pushing her away for her own good. I wasn't sure she was the type of girl who'd let herself be pushed. Maybe when this Grim business was over, I'd leave Rhode Island. Greenland was a decent place for vampires, and I'd never seen the Northern Lights.

I walked across the bridge over Interstate 195, following the zig-zag ramp leading down to the park. The red brick steps at the bottom were new since the last time I'd been there. I didn't bother following the path bordering the greenish-brown expanse of late-winter grass. The snow had mostly melted though gray and black mottled piles edged the area. India Point Park was open, with no shade, not a good place for a vampire to hang around after three in the morning. Luckily for me, it was only thirty minutes after sunset.

Blaine stood by the dock facing the water. If he shifted where he was, his nose would rest on the wood, leaving the rest of his body on the oblong lawn that hosted sunlit festivals and concerts I'd never attend. I let my boots stomp and squelch in the damp so he'd hear my approach. Even though he couldn't breathe fire in human form, I didn't want to startle him. That'd just make him regret agreeing to accept my help.

"Hey, Henry." Blaine's voice blew back over his shoulder, carried on the harbor breeze. "Fangs for joining me."

"Aww, how cute, Trogdor. That's the oldest vampire joke in the history of the English language." I stood next to him, crossing my arms in a parody of his posture.

"Knock it off, Baxter. We need to get this done pronto so I can meet everyone."

"Oh." I sighed. "It's a group outing, now?"

"Seems like you almost want Maddie out with some other guy on her own." Blaine shook his head. "What's your beef, man?"

"None." I shrugged. "I'm a vampire. Beef tastes like cardboard now."

"You poor thing. Still, you know what I mean." He gave me a sidelong glance.

"I'm not going to the shindig or hootenanny or whatever you youngsters call it." I crossed my arms over my chest.

"Not even with Maddie doing the inviting?" His eyebrow did the Mr. Spock shuffle. "I'll bet she sent your text first."

"She shouldn't have invited me. I'm bad news." I managed not to sigh by clenching my jaw.

"Oh, please. Don't tell me you're going to do the whole brooding-vampire thing. That trope's more tired than a hibernating bear shifter."

"There's a reason we brood, you know." I shook my head. Blaine couldn't possibly understand.

"Yeah, yeah. I know. The whole 'I'm dangerous, stay away from me and find a nice normal guy' thing." Blaine chuckled. I blinked, surprised because he sounded about as rueful as I felt. "I get it. I turn into a scaly beast with fiery halitosis. Almost everyone I meet is highly flammable. Danger, Will Robinson."

"So why get on my case if you get the whole threat-to-your-loved-ones thing?"

"Because it's more bull than a Minotaur. Ladies know what they want, and in this day and age, they go after it. The guy from the wrong side of wherever nobly giving up on love so the girl can 'stay good' is so 1985. Of course, you came of age then, so I shouldn't be surprised." Blaine kicked at the ground, rucking up some grass under the toe of his boot. He stared down instead of out.

"Woah, dude." I shifted my weight and put my hands on my hips. "I came to help investigate, not get dating advice."

"Package deal, my friend." Blaine turned his head, smirking at me. "You bring it, I advice it."

"Millennials." I sighed.

"Gen X-ers." Blaine's eyes rolled so far back in his head that he could probably see his brain.

"Whatever." I blew my bangs off my forehead.

"I just. Can't. " Blaine held his hands out in front of him like he held an invisible basketball.

"Are we done now?" I tapped my foot.

"Nope." Blaine dropped his hands along with the invisible basketball. "You want to help this investigation? You accept that invitation. Let the girl decide. Everybody knows you're into her. The two of you have the luxury to decide whether to date in the first place. You're lucky. Some of us, not so much."

"Fine, I'll go." I blinked. "I'll just hang out, let her choose like you said. But I've got competition now."

"It's your mind, think what you want in it." Blaine opened his backpack to reveal three familiar-looking brown paper bags on top of a pile of clothes. I realized why he'd chosen the location he had.

"Nice idea, putting them over water so they can't affect you." I stepped around to the other side of the bags, putting my back to Narragansett Bay.

"Well, if any of them have Water magic, they could." He squinted down at the bags even though he wouldn't see anything more specific than the presence of magic in human shape.

"I think that's not too likely." I put my hands on my hips.

"Well, what did you find anyway?" Blaine shook his head. "Never mind. We'll compare notes after. Stand back a little more. You don't want to be this close to me when I shift. Air displacement might knock you down."

I went where he directed. When Blaine transformed, I couldn't look away. Scraps of fabric flew around him in a nimbus before drifting back down to earth. I'd seen other shifters do their thing, but most of those were regular-sized and changed out of their clothes ahead of time. Wolves, bears, coyotes, some birds. Shifters came in all sizes, but dragons were the biggest. Blaine took up the entire lawn, and it would have been more if he hadn't doubled up his tail and kept his wings folded. His scales were reddish and edged with some lighter color. Trails of smoke curled and twisted up from nostrils the size of my hand. Blaine turned his head and blinked. A clear inner eyelid closed over the vertical slit in his orange iris, followed by an opaque scaly outer lid. When they opened again, Blaine glanced at his backpack.

I stepped closer, taking the bags out and lining them up on the deck. I tried to sense which was which. No dice. I grabbed the one to my left and opened it. Blaine stared at a spot on the deck. I peeked in, seeing immediately that I'd have to upend it carefully. Good thing there wasn't any wind that night.

The net of spider shifter silk drifted down, coming to rest on one wide wooden board. The smoke from Blaine's nostrils got thicker and whiter. If he kept that up, it'd get hard to see. I almost fell over in shock when his voice sounded in my head. I had no idea dragon shifters did telepathy. No wonder they could see magic and psychic energy. They actually used both in dragon form.

"Supernatural spyware, huh?" Blaine blinked again. I watched his eye swivel back and forth in the socket. "Imbued with Air magic, a classic choice for listening in. Where'd this come from?"

"Nocturnal Lounge, right where I work on stuff." I shrugged. "No trace of who it came from, or who built the device. Whoever imbued it was a Magus careful not to touch it and definitely not a vampire. We're just about the only people who can handle spider shifter silk without having to remove it with scissors."

"You sound like a cop." Blaine blinked with his clear lid.

"Worked with them a few times before the certification requirement." I shrugged.

"Ah." Blaine watched me put the gossamer filament back in the bag. "Next."

I tucked the bag back in Blaine's backpack and opened the next. This time, the tarot card slipped out, face down. I turned it over so Blaine could see the image of two people in love. I waited for his telepathic commentary.

"Psychically , the emotions on this make me think of lost love, but you already knew that." He opened his clear lid again. "This belongs to the Headmistress. It's got her Air magic all over it, plus a few traces from the PPC Magic Lab. She's the only one working there right now."

"Are you sure? I mean, can you tell how old the energy is?" I refused to believe Henrietta had anything to do with the attacks or the fangs. Not after the conversation we'd had on Friday. Still, she'd let the most experienced Summoner in the state go on medical leave. No. She wouldn't murder vampires, harvest their fangs, and leave them in her lab. She wasn't that evil or that stupid.

"Hmm." Blaine tilted his head, peering at the card. "Huh. Her energy is older than the lab's. That's weird." He blew a pair of smoke rings. "Where'd this one come from, do you know?"

"Crime scene. Dead vampire." I shivered.

"Tiamat's Scales." The epithet came through my mind at almost a whisper, not thundering like I expected. "Someone's trying to frame Headmistress Thurston for murder?"

"That's what I thought, too." I shook my head.

"How? You can't see the magic." He lined his left eye up with my face.

"Those emotions are all wrong for her." I didn't dare move. The background feelings coming through Blaine's telepathic link were tense and guarded. One angry breath from him and I'd be literal toast.

Now it was Blaine's turn to look at me like I was from Mars or something. His gaze would have been unsettling if he hadn't been humming the latest WBRU earworm. I wondered whether all dragon shifters used music to focus, or just Blaine. I'd have to get him listening to something better than the navel-gaze hipster stuff the local alternative station played.

"I'm not going to bother asking how or why you'd know something like that. It's pretty obvious you're about her age and this is a small state." More smoke rolled up and out of his nostrils. "I'm guessing the police aren't bothering with a formal investigation because the victim's a vampire."

"Nope. They're investigating all right." I shuddered despite my efforts not to. "A fang was found. In the PPC Magic lab. By Maddie."

"Shells of the Mother's Egg." That was just about the strongest oath a dragon shifter could invoke. "A crime against Extrahumanity? Now what I really want to know is, how'd our plucky little gaggle of college students end up with something that should be in an evidence locker?"

"Olivia's way sneakier than anyone suspects. She found these things on Lynn's hunch-based errands." I jerked my chin at the last remaining one. "I hope they give these to someone official once we're done here."

"So Josh believes." Blaine blinked. "No wonder Chief Dennison wants to meet me on Wickenden later."

"Yeah. Made a deal with him for it." I looked at my feet, the water between the deck's slats, a nail in one of the boards.

"Said deal didn't involve you avoiding a certain Umbral magus, did it?" I put the tarot card back in the bag to avoid meeting his heavy gaze.

"You're too good at guessing these things, Blaine." I sighed. "You're like the sitcom character who tells people to just kiss, already."

"Somebody's got to do it. Anyway, there's just one left. Out with it, already." He set his head back down on the edge of the deck. "Why put it off?"

I didn't tell Blaine the reasons for my reluctance. Maybe he could sense them, anyway. It felt like fear, doubt, and anticipation all joined hands in my heart to play ring-around-the-rosy. I shook my head to settle myself, then turned the last bag's contents out on the deck. The bronze amulet clinked slightly, hitting a crooked nail as it came to rest.

"Wow." Blaine raised and lowered his inner eyelids a few times. I watched his pupil widen, then narrow. The amount of scrutiny he gave the amulet made me uneasy. He even flicked his forked tongue out a few times like a snake, as though scenting with it. "This is crazy-go-nuts."

"How?"

"This amulet is designed to help suppress large amounts of magic energy. It's a little like Maddie's, and it has your Psychic energy all over it. But it's old, and has no unliving energy. So that means you made it before you got turned. And it's definitely you, not some other Memory Psychic operating at the same time. I'm comparing the energy right now, and it's an exact match except for the stuff that comes with being a vampire."

"What's that mean?"

"First of all, you're a strong Psychic. This amulet still works."

He tilted his head again, peering at me and then the amulet one more time.

"If it still works, why'd the owner get rid of it?" I raised an eyebrow.

"I can think of three reasons." Blaine flicked his tongue out again. "One, owner's dead. Maybe even the dead vampire. Two, owner figured out how to suppress their magic energy some other way. And three, which is my personal favorite because I'm paranoid. The owner wants all that magic now. They could have dropped that just so we'd know how powerful they are."

"I think you're wrong on number three, Blaine." I sighed. "I don't think villains get that mustache-twirly in the real world. You sound like Tony, not a big, bad dragon shifter."

"You're right. But that's not too surprising." Blaine's tongue flicked out again. "The big whackadoodle about this amulet isn't on the Psychic side of things. It's the magic. Whoever you bound it to has just about every type of magic energy except Unliving."

"That's impossible. No Extramagus on record has ever had that many schools of magic."

"On record. You're a Memory Psychic. You know records aren't always the whole story. They're limited. There are sealed records of Extrahuman Council trials where the only things on file are a case number and a memory amulet. One of these from back during Prohibition was about an Extramagus, actually. The identity was sealed, something about protecting the family from the sins of the forebear. This Extramagus had a physical limitation—paraplegia. Kept trying to get turned to keep all that magic and lose the limitation. When the vampires refused, he started picking them off during the day. Extrahuman Council agreed to take him out. I only know about it because my mom was part of that squad."

"So how come I don't remember making this?"

"No idea. There are too many ways you might have forgotten." Blaine turned his head to put his eye next to my face again. "Some of them might even incriminate you."

"You mean I might have agreed to wipe my own memory, or let the Extramagus do it with Mind magic? Not as incriminating as you might think. I agree to that kind of thing all the time. Keep a stash of amulets hidden away. Evidence galore in case someone decides to screw me over later." I sighed. "All I'd need is time to go through them."

"So the right amulet might tell us exactly who the Extramagus is?"

"Yup." I straightened, finally feeling like I might be useful in this whole mess.

"And there's a whole new reason you're the target, my friend." Blaine blinked slowly with his outer lid. "You might be able to out this Extramagus at any time."

"Not really." I sighed. "The thing is, I don't remember which amulet is which. It could take months to find the right one. Years even."

"Then start working on that as soon as you can." Blaine blew three more smoke rings before thinking at me again. "If you helped the Extramagus before, that explains why it's a Summoner attacking you now. Big bad Extramagus has to use a cat's paw. Get the clothes out of my bag, please. It's time to shift back, and I don't want to get arrested for indecent exposure."

I nodded and dragged out stacks of Blaine's not-so-neatly folded clothing. Then, I repacked the amulet. I didn't have to look up to know Blaine had shifted back. The surrounding air got cooler and felt emptier without the huge dragon on the lawn. I zipped the bag, waiting until the rustle of fabric ceased before standing and looking up. Blaine shouldered his backpack.

"Hey, wait, what's this?" Blaine trotted over to the edge of the deck. He rolled one sleeve all the way up his arm, then reached down to the water.

I approached, watching him fish something round and about

the size of a bocce ball out of the flotsam on the water's surface. It glimmered faintly with a naggingly familiar iridescent energy. Blaine turned around, pulled a small towel out of the front of his backpack, then wiped the orb.

"What is it?" I scratched my head. I couldn't remember seeing anything like it before, and the strange energy had me puzzled.

"Japanese sea float. Kelpies, Selkies, and Tanuki think they're lucky. Can't hurt to have in a pinch, even though I don't know anyone who can use Faerie and Water magic." He passed it to me. "Check it out."

"What's that weird haze around it? Not the magic, the other golden glowy stuff?" I turned it over, watching its energy swirl and twist over and around the other magic like an oil slick, only much more pleasant-looking.

"Gold, you say?" Blaine raised an eyebrow. "Sounds like luck energy. That's something I can't verify without shifting back, and we're out of time and wardrobe for that sort of thing. I'll check into it tomorrow or something."

"Okay." I peered at the sea float, then handed it back and let Blaine stow it under the paper bags. The object held me transfixed in a state of fascination until Blaine zipped up his backpack.

"Let's meet Chief Dennison and go have fun, old man." Blaine slapped me on the shoulder, snapping me out of my reverie. He strode away across the winter-yellowed grass, breath puffing out of his mouth in the cold. The fact he was a dragon added to the volume of vapor trailing behind us as we crossed the bridge. I could almost pretend I was really alive.

We headed down the ramp on the Fox Point side. When we got to the street, Blaine waited. A PPC Campus Police car pulled up, and the window rolled down. The guy inside looked a lot like Josh, but older and with a buzz cut instead of a spiky hairdo. He asked for the bags.

"Here you go, Chief Dennison." Blaine set his backpack on the passenger seat, unzipped it, and let the Chief take the three bags out.

"I expect a formal report from each of you by tomorrow afternoon." He looked straight ahead instead of at either of us. "Bring it in-person."

"No problem." Blaine pulled his backpack back through the window and waved. I just nodded even though Chief Dennison hadn't looked at me once.

CHAPTER FOURTEEN

Maddie

"Yes, Mom. I'm actually going out with people who remember me." I spritzed my hair with just a little water, wanting my curls to perk up, not freeze.

"That's awesome!" Mom's squeal made me jump and squirt my face instead. I even heard her hands clap in the background.

"Mom, your eighties is showing." After patting my face dry, I gave my eyeliner an appraising look. I'd have to fix it now.

"I don't care." She lowered her voice and cleared her throat. "Is it a guy? It's a guy, right?" She reminded me of the seagulls in Finding Nemo.

"Yeah, Mom." I sighed. "There's a guy."

"Oh, now that doesn't sound like something you're happy about." She clicked her tongue against her teeth. "What's wrong?"

"It's just *a* guy, not *the* guy."

"Oh. Sounds disappointing." I could picture her, pulling at one of her springy curls and letting it go. I'd ended up with a hair type somewhere in between her tight, natural curls and Dad's straight, thick tresses.

"It is." I rummaged in my cosmetic bag for my eyeliner. "This guy, when he asked me out, it was like he had to or something."

"Then don't go." I heard the clink of a teacup on a saucer. Even out of town, Mom always settled in with a book and a cup of oolong. "Don't put up with that, Maddie. You deserve better."

"I know." I uncapped the liner. It'd only take a few seconds to fix the smudge. "I invited friends along, so I don't care that Josh is being weird."

"Wait. Which one's Josh?" When I heard Mom's tiny gasp, I pictured her clutching the front of the robe she'd tie-dyed herself before I was born. My mother was too earthy-crunchy to clutch pearls. She said flannel was just fine for her, thank-you-very-much. "He's not the fellow I hired to make your amulet, is he?"

"No, Mom." I blinked, nearly poking myself in the eye with the brush. I don't mess around with a pencil for that. Liquid all the way. As I braced my elbow on the counter, the real meaning of my mother's words sank in. "Did you see something about Henry?"

"Sweetie, I couldn't tell you if I did." Her sigh might have carried wistfulness over Mount Everest if it hadn't come through the phone first.

"Yeah. I figured it had something to do with your Precognition." I fixed the line on my upper lid and put the brush back in the bottle, twisting the cap. "Josh is a wolf shifter. Kind of Alpha-jerky, but does the right thing most of the time. His dad runs Campus Police."

"And he's the indifferent asker-outer?" She muffled the slight slurp as she sipped tea.

"Yeah. I think someone put him up to it." I chuckled, so she'd think it wasn't a big deal, but that effort fell flatter than a pancake from the Empire State Building.

"Lame." Mom clicked her tongue again. "And yes, I did say that back when I was your age."

"It applies." I had to get her off her tangent. "Mom, I called to ask you something serious, and you've avoided it the whole time we've been on the phone."

"Okay." I heard the rustle and rattle of cards being shuffled. "What's your question again?"

"Mom, put the cards down. I don't want a tarot answer, just a Mom one. It's not about the future."

"Oh?" I heard a hollow thud as she set her deck down. I could almost see her, leaning on her elbow in a mirror-image of the posture I used to apply all the makeup she never bothered with. Her brown eyes would be slightly unfocused, traveling the room until they rested on her deck again. "Fine, then ask away, sweetie."

"Mom, why hasn't Dad turned you?"

"Why didn't you tell me it was a personal question?" She was dodgier than cat-form Tony in a room full of rocking chairs for some reason.

"Oh, come on, Mom. Please just answer me." Her side of the family had Changeling blood, so sometimes it was hard to get a direct answer out of her. Other times, she just spouted things I wished I could unhear. Life with a precog was interesting.

"It's not time yet."

"Have you ever thought that if you wait much longer, you won't get the license approved before it's too late? They can take decades to finalize, Mom, you know that."

"We already have the license. Had it since you started Kindergarten."

"Wait, what? Then why aren't you turned already?" I spritzed my hair with water again. Yay, speaker-phone.

"Like I said, it's not time yet. Close, but we need to wait a little longer."

"What are you waiting for, Haley's Comet? Another solar eclipse?"

"Nothing like that." She sighed. "I can't tell you yet, either. Don't feel bad. No one knows why, except me and Dad."

"Oh. It's one of those thingamabobs." I snapped my fingers, trying to remember the word. "A psychic whatsis. Starts with the letter c, I think?"

"Yes. A contingency." I heard the clink of stone on stone. She'd be charging her crystals since I'd asked her to put down her cards. "If I mention the thing I'm waiting for, it might never happen."

"Yeah. Oh, and thanks. I passed a test because I know so much about coincidence and contingency. I told Professor Thurston I owe it all to you."

"Sorry I can't tell you, but we've got what we need." She sounded more relaxed now that I'd dropped the subject. "Your grandma used to think we'd split up if I kept waiting."

"I learned last semester how the turnings during the Big Reveal split a lot of families up." I put the spray bottle back in my bag. "You and Dad are outliers, you know. Weird, huh?"

"There's nothing wrong with that, Maddie, especially when you're both happy. If something improves your life, helps you feel cared for and less alone, then it's right for you. When a place or person makes you feel like that, it's a keeper."

"Thanks, Mom." I packed my makeup away. "I have to go now, meet people."

"Well, thanks for calling. I always love hearing your voice." Her voice brightened instantly. "Have a good time!"

"I think I just might now, Mom." I picked up the phone and tapped the icon to turn off the speaker. "Love you."

"I love you too, sweetie." She hung up.

I walked down the empty hall to my room. After I'd put away my cosmetics and hooked my phone to the charger, I glanced over at Lynn's side of the room. She'd found someone and gone for it, even though she spent the better part of last semester thinking she couldn't make friends.

I'd spent the better part of my life thinking no one would remember me long enough to care the way Dad and Mom cared for each other. Last semester, I'd asked Lynn to stick around at PPC because hope was important and she was worth it. It was time to follow my own advice.

The intercom buzzed just as I started scrolling through my phone contacts to find Henry's number. I set the phone down and pressed the intercom button.

"Hello?" It had to be for Lynn.

"Hi, Maddie." Nox's voice surprised me. Should she be able to remember me?

"Nox. What's up?" Of course, she'd remember. She had Faerie magic.

"Figured I'd walk over with you if that's okay?"

"Sure." I pushed the button to open the door downstairs. "Fifth floor. Meet me in the lounge. Left off the elevator, you can't miss it."

"Cool, thanks." I heard the door downstairs open over the static-filled connection, then let go of the intercom button.

I put my wallet and keys in a smaller satchel than the one I carried to class. I added lipstick, my spray bottle, and the Umbral Affinity book. Brodsky could send the Brownie after us. It couldn't do much to hurt us, but it could spy and try roping people into bargains. Water might scare it off. It'd be able to sense the trail of my magic if I hid after it saw me, but the book might have some tips on how to mitigate that.

Nox was already in the lounge when I got there. I'd called Henry, but he hadn't answered, so I sat next to Nox, tapping my foot. I stopped that as soon as I noticed. There had to be a reason he hadn't picked up, right? A reason that didn't involve some kind of attack or disaster. The sun had set almost a half-hour earlier. I glanced at my phone, then away again.

"Waiting for a message?" She tilted her head, a slight smile tilting the corners of her mouth.

"Maybe." I shrugged.

"I'd be worried, too." She nodded.

"Huh?" I blinked.

"About whoever you're messaging. We were like Captain Obvious and his In-your-face Band of Obviosity Pirates over at Brodsky's."

"Yeah, I was just thinking about that when you got here." I pulled opened my satchel, showing her the spray bottle. "Check it out, brownie repellent." She laughed.

"Josh and I have big red targets painted on our backs now." Nox smirked, eyes sparkling. I only just noticed she wasn't wearing her Kelpie skin. "Trouble with a capital T. T is for taunt, drawing aggro for you guys."

"You say that like it's a good thing to pull the boss without your armor." It was my turn to laugh. I got the reference even though I'd stopped playing World of Warcraft a few years back.

"Maybe it is. It might take the heat off Henry long enough for him to figure something out. He's the one with psychometry, right?"

"It's a little like psychometry, but really he's reading old memories."

"Isn't that the same thing?"

"Not really. A Psychometry Psychic can touch something another person hasn't and still get an impression. It'd be all about the object and its history. Henry can't read something unless someone touched it. And what he gets has to do with the person who touched it, not really the object."

"Wow, you know a lot about Psychics." She raised her eyebrows.

"My parents are Psychics."

"Cool. We have Magi in our family. I was born mundane,

though, so that's why I got the pelt instead of my brother. He's an Earth Magus."

"Wow." I wasn't sure what that meant, but Nox seemed to be in an explanatory mood.

"Yeah. Incompatible magic. It'd be amazing to have both if they didn't cancel each other out, though."

"Yeah, it'd be like a Magus with more than one school who could also shift. And had Faerie powers."

"Totally broken." She smirked. "GM would hit it with the nerf bat."

We laughed together, then stopped when my phone beeped. The screen said **Josh Dennison** instead of **Henry Baxter**. The corners of my mouth dropped like rocks.

"Not who you wanted to hear from, huh?" Nox didn't even try looking at my phone. My level of respect for her skyrocketed.

"No." I checked the message. *Here already, where r u?* I sighed. "Let's go. Josh is already at the cafe. Lynn, Bobby, Blaine, and Tony are going to meet us there. Maybe Henry." I tried to look as nonchalant as possible. "Olivia decided she needs sleep more than a night out."

"Is she really a diurnal owl shifter?" Nox pushed the lounge door open.

"Better living through chemistry." I ducked under her arm and out into the hall. "You should meet her sometime. She's read just about everything in the universe. Remembers it all, too. Like a walking trivia bank."

"So you're saying she's a hoot?"

We laughed together all the way down the stairs. I'm not exactly sure why Nox headed for the stairwell instead of the elevator, but I didn't mind five flights down. Up would have been another story with my short legs. Outside, I saw a familiar long, black car standing at the curb in front of the building. As we started walking by, the window rolled down.

"Mr. Harcourt sent me to drive you to Wickenden Street."

Nox blinked and stared at the liveried driver. I didn't blame her. The chauffeur was like a movie trope, with a shiny hat, white gloves, and a pristine uniform.

"Blaine's the only person I know whose family has more money than the Dennisons. It's legit."

"Okay, then." She reached for the door, but the driver shook his head, got out of the car, and did it for her. "Swanky." She climbed in. "I never imagined."

"I haven't been in one either." After I got in, I bounced a little to test the springy, plush seats.

Nox sat across from me, long legs stretched out in front of her. I seriously envied her shiny oil-slick leggings. I'd never have the guts to wear those without a skirt over them. She put one hand over her mouth, giggling at my antics. I found a radio and switched it on. NPR talk. I rolled my eyes and pulled a cord out of my bag. Once one end was plugged into my phone, I connected the other to a jack next to the radio. A few swipes and taps got us some decent music. Peter Murphy's voice crooned about how Bela Lugosi was dead. Undead, undead, undead.

"Wow, this is an old song." Nox shut her eyes and swayed. "My mom loved this stuff."

"Mine didn't. She's kind of a hippie." I chuckled. "Listens to Jimi Hendricks, Fleetwood Mac, Janis Joplin. She and my dad both wonder where I got the Post-Punk bug."

"You never told them?"

"I'm not sure myself." I shrugged. "Just that when I heard this kind of music, the first thing I thought of was my shadows. This stuff sounds like how they feel."

"After being in them myself, I can see why."

The car stopped. I put my cord away, and we got out. The cafe was half a block down. We thanked the driver and walked over. Josh opened the door. He held it, standing with his back against it as we passed. He barely looked at me because his eyes were glued to Nox. It was nice to see my new friend getting some attention, but downright weird that he'd asked me out when she'd been standing right there. Hopefully, he'd rectify that and leave me alone, already. All I could think while he held the door was how he'd unknowingly left the house in a shirt with the "f" word all over it.

The scent of coffee and wood polish surrounded me like a warm hug. I remembered how Henry said he loved the smell of coffee. Lynn and Bobby leaned together on a less threadbare couch than the one at Professor Brodsky's. Tony sat on an ottoman which didn't match the chairs. They waved us over. I plunked myself down in a chair-and-a-half, leaning on the arm so no one could share it with me. The only comfy seats left were two spots on a loveseat. Josh pulled a hard wooden chair over from one table, turned it around, and straddled it. Nox took the love seat, stretching her legs out under the coffee table. I watched Lynn's left eyebrow do its Spock imitation at the seating shuffle. She opened her mouth to say something snarky, but Bobby's impromptu shoulder massage put a stop to that.

"What do you want?" Josh propped his elbow on the chair back, then leaned his chin on his fist. His eyes focused on a spot somewhere between Nox and me.

"Coffee, black like my soul." I spoke in a sing-song voice with the brightest smile I could manage. Tony burst out laughing, Bobby joined in, and Lynn chuckled behind her hair.

"Light and bitter for me." Nox smiled across at Josh, her expression somewhere between flirtatious and predatory. "That's exactly what I like."

Josh got up and turned toward the counter pretty fast, but I still noticed his reddening cheeks. Once he was up there, Lynn put her serious face back on and gave me a pointed look. I smiled and shrugged. She lifted her eyebrows and shrugged back.

"Hey, look who decided to show up!" Tony stood smiling at the door. I turned to see who was there.

Blaine and Henry shouldered into the shop. I watched Henry

inhale through his nose, his eyes going half-lidded just as I'd imagined. I shifted my weight to make room in the chair, kicking myself for choosing the smaller seat. Blaine made a beeline for the other half of the loveseat, plunking himself down next to Nox. He smiled at me.

"This is your friend from lab, right, Maddie?"

"Yes. Blaine, this is Nox. Nox, Blaine."

"Thanks for sending your car around, even though it was ostentatiously swanky."

"I'll need it over here for later, anyway." He gave Nox a toothy grin. "My walk was much shorter. It was the least I could do. And everyone should get to ride in one at some point. Same goes for other kinds of rides."

While Blaine played out his particular brand of not really humble demurral and flirtation, I looked for Henry. He was at the counter, speaking to Josh in low tones. Both had their hands on their hips. I wondered what they were arguing about, so I tried reading their lips.

"It didn't work." Josh clenched his jaw, shaking his head. "It's like trying to mix up oil and water."

"So, now what?" Henry shifted his weight from one foot to the other.

"Go." Josh jerked his chin at the door.

"Blaine brought me. He won't like that." He raised an eyebrow.

"Tough." Josh crossed his arms over his chest, tucking his chin to hide his throat. He stared directly into Henry's eyes. I knew an Alpha stare when I saw one. "You said you'd quit."

"I did." Henry smirked.

"She didn't." Josh sneered.

"Tough." It was Henry's turn to cross his arms, though he didn't tuck his chin.

I stood. They had no right to talk like I couldn't make my own decisions. As I stepped around the love-seat, Blaine glanced up. He winked, then gave me a sly little smirk. I tilted my head, raising an eyebrow. He responded by jerking his chin at the vampire/werewolf standoff and waving one hand at me in a "move along" gesture. I went. Henry was already out the door by the time I got to Josh.

"Don't go to all this trouble on my account, Josh." I immediately crossed my arms and tucked my chin, glaring up at him with upturned eyes. "I'll determine my own dating prospects."

"He's dangerous, Maddie." Josh met my eyes, reminding me of half the arguments I'd seen on TV between brothers and sisters.

"So am I. Umbral magic's no joke." I gestured at myself. "Poison hides in pretty bottles."

"Prove you can handle him and I'll get out of your way." He glared down his nose at me.

I focused my energy, marking an invisible circle around Josh's head. Then, I filled it with shadow. I heard Blaine's voice choking out choice words about Tiamat. I glanced over my shoulder where the rest of the group looked puzzled with one other notable exception. Tony. How in the world could he see magic? That was a question for another time. I peered back through my shadows at Josh. He turned his head, nostrils flaring as he scented the air. His head cocked to either side, ears wiggling slightly as he listened. He got nothing, of course. The sphere of shadow had cut off all of his senses except direct touch.

"Proven." The rest of Josh's breath whooshed out in a relieved sigh. "Now knock it off."

I called back my magic, smirking up at him. His slight frown upended itself, spreading out into an easy smile. Josh dropped his arms to his sides.

"Let's go bring him back." Josh turned toward the door.

"No, I got this." I shook my head, hoping my bouncy curls didn't make me look like an intractable toddler.

"Nothing doing. I'm responsible for this whole business." Josh narrowed his eyes.

"So am I, and—" Just as I was about to break the truce and call

Josh a third-wheel, I heard a feminine gasp and a low male chuckle. Over on the love-seat, Blaine had turned on the charm. He was putting some serious moves on Nox, one arm around her shoulders as he grinned. He smiled, then turned a challenging glance on Josh. So that's what he'd meant with all the pantomime. I felt like I was stuck in a production of As You Like It.

"Handle it yourself, then." Josh's eyes glimmered. He handed me the black coffee. Now, Josh had something more important than a brooding vampire on his mind. He strode over to the rest of the group, turning his back on me.

I headed out of the cafe, glancing through the window to see Josh approach the love-seat, then stop. He'd forgotten Nox's coffee. Blaine got up to get it. Lynn and Bobby looked on in confusion. Tony grinned like he was from Cheshire, knowing he'd have some extremely juicy gossip for Monday.

Once on the street, I shut my eyes. I couldn't track the unliving energy that made Henry what he was, but I had my amulet. I reached in my shirt and focused on the connection between it and me, the one he'd helped me make. After that, it was easy. I ended up in front of the Wickenden Pub. Ninety-nine beers, one sign said. I read another one: Top Ten Reasons You'll Not Feel You Belong at the Wickenden Pub.

I smiled and went in.

CHAPTER FIFTEEN

Henry

I stared at the scarred table, not realizing what was carved in the wood next to the unfortunately, sweating glass that contained my stout. I'd nearly forgotten that the Wickenden Pub served all their beer cold. While drawing a line down the condensation with my pinkie, I sighed. I dragged water through the letters H and T. That was when I remembered why the x under the initials hadn't been a mistake. Rick had meant to make a multiplication sign between Henrietta's initials and his. He'd wanted a whole tribe of children with her back when we celebrated his twenty-first. All he had to wait for, he'd said, was her graduation.

But Henrietta had kept going and going, like an academic Energizer Bunny, until she had two Ph.Ds. I remember waiting and watching for birth announcements in the paper after Rick exiled me from our social circle, finding nothing. Even though they wanted nothing to do with me, I still cared about them. Back in 1999, hospitals were the only place to get legal blood. When I'd seen Henrietta over at Women and Infants, crying on the shoulder of a nurse with a Maternity Ward badge, I understood. Some things weren't in the cards for everyone.

The Wickenden Pub smelled like beer, stale beer, and old pizza with a slight hint of bathroom disinfectant that got stronger the closer you sat to the back exit. That's why the trace of myrrh and jasmine puzzled me. I had to stop thinking about Maddie so much, even though I'd never be able to forget her. I'd been an idiot, making an impression of her like that. I should have known it'd come back to bite me.

The warm hand covering mine was a total surprise. I looked up, so startled I almost knocked over my untouched stout. She steadied the glass, then picked it up and took a sip. She grimaced.

"Ugh. Why do they serve it cold?" Maddie stuck her tongue out, closing one eye.

"Maddie, go back to the cafe." I closed my eyes. She was still there when I opened them.

"Wow." The round O of her mouth broadened into a hard smile. "Just so we're clear, I don't take orders from baby Alphas or vampires who idolize Buffy The Vampire Slayer's boyfriends."

"Are you challenging me?" I raised an eyebrow.

"You think you're Josh's Beta or something?" She smirked.

"Ask him." I shrugged.

"You'll need this, then." She pulled what looked like a half-dollar on a string out of her pocket, plunking it on the table between us.

"An alliance amulet?" I'd never seen one before. "Where did you get this?"

"Lab. It was the second thing I fished out of that box. Nice little coincidence, huh?"

"No such thing as a nice coincidence." The phrase was automatic. I hadn't intended to lead her on at all, at least not consciously. I recognized the defeatism in that line of thinking.

"Most of the time, you're wrong." She rubbed the side of my

hand with her thumb. Why hadn't I shaken off her touch? "Coincidence is the only protection anyone has from a Magus. Resist enough times, you're safe. What tends to happen the most keeps on happening when magic affects people."

"I'm not exactly people anymore, Maddie." I shook my head.

"Magic Theory says you are. So do I."

I didn't say anything. I could try to argue with her, but she had the Magic Theory facts right. Coincidence meant that all Extrahumans had more concrete confirmation of sentience than anything the humans had come up with. The Extrahuman Rights trials had set a precedent for using magical tenets to help define our legal rights. A Brownie or a Djinn would fall under those rules, for example. The Grim wouldn't.

"Listen, Henry, because I'm only going to say this once. I'm falling in love with you. I don't think there's a way to stop it, and I don't want to, anyway. You've done a whole world of good here, and I have a feeling you could go on to do even more. I want to be there with you for all of it."

"I'm a vampire, Maddie. You already have to deal with one person in your life living like a second-class citizen. I don't want you to have to deal with one more."

"You'll make two more, actually. Mom has a license for turning."

"Then things will already be hard enough for you in the near future."

"I don't think so. This right here," she tapped the medallion, "represents an old traditions of belonging and respect. That tradition went on for ages. The way society treats vampires now will pass, eventually. The world will see that you're like any other people, with the potential for horror or honor. Honor won most of the time back in the day until technically immortal people had to worry about death. It'll win again, if only you expect it of yourself and let people appreciate it when they see it on you."

"That doesn't happen very often."

"I think the hostess over at Luxe Burger would disagree."

"The opinion the two of you share about me is an unpopular one."

"But it's not wrong. And if you don't let people express it, no one with the wrong idea will ever know about the right one." Maddie's grin was gentle when I'd expected smug. She had me with that argument. Be the change you want to see.

"And what idea is that?"

"Just the slightly unhinged notion that any type of Extrahuman is part of humanity. It's right there in the term, after all. We're all worthy of dignity, respect, belonging. And love." She squeezed my hand. "Especially that. No one should have to resign themselves to eternity alone. Especially a man who can't forget."

"Heady stuff from the woman no one remembers."

"I'm afraid. Someday, I'll be alone forever and no one will remember me." Her smile dimmed down, darkening with the loneliness that hounded her as tenaciously as any Grim.

"Look, most people can't remember you, but you've been here just over six months and already found a score who want to." I took the alliance amulet off the table, pocketing it. After all the decades of change and danger I'd been through, it was time to let my guard down.

"Maddie, you control your actions, how you treat people. You could be awful to the lot of us, lie about what actually happened, hide things we need as a prank. If you were that kind of person, all the memory enhancements and coincidence in the world wouldn't make any difference. That's all on you. Only some of your fate gets decided by coincidence. The rest is a choice."

"Unless it intersects with a contingency." Her eyes widened suddenly like she'd just had a eureka moment. I watched her shake inspiration off. "Oh!" She blinked at something over my shoulder. "Don't turn around. Act natural."

"What is it?" I kept gazing at her.

"Brodsky's Brownie."

"What do Russian baked goods have to do with anything?"

"Professor Brodsky." She leaned close to my ear and lowered her voice. "The Summoner. He had a Brownie guarding his apartment."

"Wait, you went there?" I murmured back, finally at ease with being this close to her.

"Yeah. With Nox and Josh." She drummed her fingers on the table.

"Oh. What should we do?"

"Get out of here. Try to shake the Brownie so I can hide us."

"Why not hide us now?"

"If they see me cast, they'll track the spell."

"Okay, then. We walk out through the back. Pretend you're on the way to the restroom. I'll follow you in a minute."

"Fine." She leaned in and kissed me. This time, it didn't last nearly long enough.

I watched Maddie walk past the scarred tables, ratty chairs, and long, dark bar to the far end of the room. The narrow hallway had a sign over it that said Restrooms. Her nose wrinkled, then she stepped into the darkened hallway and out of sight. I picked up my stout and chugged it down without worrying. It couldn't make me drunk or even tipsy. The taste was barely there, like anything a vampire drinks cold. Maybe the next time I tried drinking alcohol for taste, it should be Irish Coffee or something.

I picked up the empty glass and stared into it, letting my shoulders droop to put on a good show for the brownie. Then, I shrugged at no one in particular and brought the glass back over to the bar. By this hour, it was crowded and dark enough for me to blend in. No one else had a jacket with smeared white paint on the back, but that wouldn't make me stand out in the barroom murk. I set the glass at the far end of the counter, then squeezed past some kids who could only be from the Rhode Island School of Design. They could give Blaine's hoity a run for its toity. The guys had beards and pompadour hairdos atop tight flannel shirts, suspenders, and skinny jeans. The girls wore a mosh pit of pastel colors screen-printed with birds and feathers.

"Hey, buddy!" One of the guys called out to me. I looked over my shoulder at him. "Haven't you heard Bela Lugosi's dead?"

"Yeah. Undead." I gave him a smile to shame the day-star.

I ignored the surprised noises they made and the air of their backward passage as they all scrambled to avoid me. One of them looked past me and did a double-take. He'd seen the Brownie, but the tilt of his head told me the Faerie was still at the front of the pub.

The hallway was a malodorous new world. People should be full of piss and vinegar, not my nostrils. I didn't have to breathe, but the ghost of the Wickenden Pub's bathrooms would haunt me for at least five minutes of outdoor walking. I didn't have much reason to pray anymore but gave thanks that the Grim couldn't be summoned for four more days. That beast could smell us from a mile away.

I pushed through the door outside. At first, I didn't spot Maddie at the back of the courtyard. She stood near the corner where the wall was lowest. I'd forgotten there wasn't an exit back here. The staff wouldn't want people using the back patio to skip out on their bills. The wall was an easy jump for me. I could tell right away Maddie didn't think she'd make it over.

"We'll have to jump it."

"I can't." Her curls bounced when she shook her head, eyes glimmering with imminent tears.

"Sure, you can." I glanced over my shoulder.

"Nope, no way." I noticed her shivering. She shouldn't have been since it wasn't too cold for her warm jacket.

"Okay, I get it." I lifted her in my arms, trying not to get lost in the rush of emotion as her body pressed against mine. It'd been decades since I'd done anything that felt this heroic. "You're scared of heights.

"Caught me. I'm not perfect."

"Good. Neither am I."

I jumped to the top of the wall, planting my feet firmly to absorb the shock with my knees. Here's where the extra strength and durability from being a vampire helped. Usually, a law-abiding person like me didn't leap too many walls. At the top, I looked down. Good thing I hadn't vaulted completely over and into the throng of trash cans behind the Pub.

I trotted along the top of the wall easily. Better balance was another vampiric perk. How had I forgotten I could do all this? Had I really been too scared and miserable to have any simple fun? I jumped down, setting Maddie on her feet. She adjusted her shirt and jacket, then smiled up at me.

"That was kind of cool, but only because I didn't look down." She closed her eyes and stepped back into the shadow of the wall, then leaned against it. I joined her, listening while she murmured the same words she'd used in the tunnels under the library. Shadows gathered around us. We'd be hidden now.

"Heh. Maybe we'll do it again sometime." I held out my hand, and she took it, walking back toward campus. I didn't want to drop her off at home. Maybe we should stay out.

Maddie tugged my hand. I stopped, looking down at her face full of fear. She stared across the street. This was a night of firsts for me. The creature peering through the shadows was a Spite.

I'd only seen a sketch of one. When a Sprite displeased the Sidhe Queen, she'd turn them into a hunting hound. Their wings became prehensile spikes with stingers on the ends, which could paralyze even vampires and dragon shifters. Spites could see magic because they ate it. If the Spite caught up with Maddie, they'd drink her magic. She'd only get her power back if she got away before a complete drain.

Spites were summonable like Grims and Brownies, but the Summoner needed a Seelie oath, tithe, or fealty in order to control it accurately. That meant either Brodsky or the Extramagus was hooked up with the Queen's Court.

"We have to get someplace safe." I racked my brain, trying to think of something.

"Needs a physical barrier." Maddie was right. Spites eat wards.

"Yup. Do we run?" As a Psychic, I didn't have much to fear from them. Unless they'd had been given orders to stake and behead me, of course.

"Not from a Spite. The faster you go when they can see you, the stronger they get. Walk like a normal person."

We continued up the street and the hill. I couldn't think. We had to get somewhere fortified. Magi warded places instead of buying good locks, including most buildings on campus. If I got through all this, I'd be having a talk with Josh about the common-sense of mundane locks. There'd be no shelter anywhere on campus with the Nocturnal Lounge still under construction.

I headed for my apartment. If it'd keep Maddie safe long enough for the Spite's time or energy to run out, I'd take it. My building was old, so I'd risk it trying to dig through the brick. But if the Spite broke through after sunrise that'd be the end of me. It'd take most of the Spite's time to do it, though, so it couldn't get Maddie after that. My landlord would be pissed, but I wouldn't be around to get evicted, anyway.

I bolted the front door and the basement door, then rushed downstairs with Maddie in tow. The Spite must be padding around outside of the building on feet with opposable thumbs. That was one of the creepiest things about them. The Sidhe Queen turned the Sprite into a killing machine, leaving just enough sentience to make victims pity it as they died. Have you ever seen a mastiff in pain? I learned that night that a Spite's eyes look like that all the time. I turned the key in the deadbolt, then followed Maddie into my tiny apartment.

"Don't worry, I'll get the lights after I lock the door." I threw the deadbolt, then did the chains and latches at the top and bottom of the door.

"Won't just shutting it work? I mean, it opens out so the Spite can't batter it down." Maddie's voice came from somewhere behind me and to the left. I turned on the lights just in time to stop her from tripping over one of the chairs and into the table.

"They can work latches and doorknobs, but can't pick locks." My fangs pricked my lower lip. I hadn't realized how hungry I was. But how had I used that much energy jumping on and off a silly little wall and doing up locks at Extrahuman speeds?

"I was afraid you'd say that." She set her satchel on the table, then took her jacket off and hung it on the back of the chair she'd almost tripped over. All I could smell was her blood.

"I have a book on pure Seelie creatures if you want to look at it to pass the time." I headed straight for the fridge and opened it. Nothing. I couldn't understand. I'd just stocked up at the Providence Animal Rescue League on Wednesday. I always got a week's supply. There should be at least five bags in there. Where could they be?

"I can think of other things I'd rather do." Her voice didn't sound low, purring, or husky. I had to hope she didn't have anything physical in mind.

"Um—" Before I could protest, Maddie crossed away from me.

"I haven't seen this much vinyl ever." She looked over my music collection with her back to me. I leaned against my empty refrigerator, unsure whether I'd be able to stay on the other side of the room from her. "Is it okay if I play a couple of these? I've never seen some of these EPs and imports."

"Go ahead." The words came out slightly slurred. Vampires always have fangs, but the hungrier we get, the more they stick out. They were at an awkward length for speaking by then.

Maddie froze with her hand hovering in the air next to a Siouxsie and the Banshees record. She looked over her shoulder and narrowed her eyes. Then, she stepped slowly sideways, crossing the short distance between the records to my bookshelf.

Without turning her back to me, Maddie eased out the book on pure Seelies. She checked the index, flipping through some pages. Her eyes flicked from side to side across the pages, slower than her brainiac roommate's but still respectably quickly. When they stopped, her eyes widened and her eyebrows went up.

"Henry, you're in trouble."

"Yeah, I know." I shut my eyes, trying not to look at her to stop thinking about biting her. I opened them, realizing that only made it worse. With my eyes closed, all I could hear and smell were her heartbeat and blood. "I don't know why."

"The Spite drains all kinds of magical energy. When you feed, the blood you take turns into Unliving magic. That's why it fuels you. When we walked here, you got between me and it. Must have been just close enough for it to steal a bunch of what keeps you going."

"I did not know they could do that." After all the times I'd complained about going back to school, I finally understood why the Licensure Board required it. Too bad I'd be dead in the morning.

"Well, the good news is, it can't do it until it can see you. So when you get a snack from the fridge, you'll be all set."

"It's empty."

"Move over." I stepped in front of the sink, letting Maddie wrinkle her nose and furrow her brow at half my kitchen. She shooed me away from that, too. After looking back and forth a bunch of times between the sink and the refrigerator, she nodded. "Water magic with little tiny foot and hand-prints. I just saw that in the book. Pixie. Looks like Brodsky has quite the crew at his beck and call."

"I don't understand." I shook my head, moving back in front of the sink again. "What's Brodsky got against PPC or vampires or us in particular?"

"Don't know. Maybe call Lynn and Blaine about that?" Maddie flipped through the book again. "Pixies. They're tiny, elemental, and summonable. They could get in through the sinks." She headed to the bathroom, looking over her shoulder before going in. "I'm warding the faucets."

"Good idea." I sat down at the table across from Maddie's jacket and tried not to think. With the Spite outside, she couldn't run from the hungry vampire inside. Coming to my apartment had been a bad idea. It was too small for me to get far enough away from my temptation. What made it worse was I felt exactly the same way Maddie did. I was falling in love.

Vampires had the drive to turn people they loved, especially someone who'd be genetically compatible afterward. After Death Magi, Umbral were most likely to be. And Maddie had grown up with a turned dad, meaning she'd been exposed to more than enough of the right kind of magic. Within just a couple of hours, I'd barely be able to control myself. If I turned her without a permit, she'd be lucky to spend eternity in prison. I'd be executed.

"That's everything. There's only one thing left to do." Maddie stepped away from the counter. I'd been so lost in thought I hadn't noticed her warding spell.

"Yup. Go open the top drawer of my dresser." I watched her cross the room, nearly mesmerized by the steady, strong pulse under the smooth skin on her neck.

"Stakes?" She raised one eyebrow.

"You have to use one. It's the only way I won't go nuts and try to turn you in a couple of minutes."

"Not the only way. If that Spite or anything else breaks in here and you're staked, they'll take your head, and that's the end for both of us. We'll need to be able to protect each other." She dropped the stake back in the drawer and closed it. Then, she pulled her sweater over her head, draping it over her jacket as she approached me. "You won't be at full power with what I can give, but this way we won't have to fight each other or leave you paralyzed. Relax. My mom and dad do this all the time."

"Maddie, we shouldn't." I shook my head. "I haven't done this all the time. All my blood came from bags or donors who used knives. I've never even bitten anyone before."

"Huh." She put her hands over my shoulders, gripping the back of the chair behind them. "I've never been bitten either."

By then, I couldn't say anything else. She'd draped herself across my lap, leaning against me in a way that reminded me of leaping the wall. Had I really felt like a hero then, like something more than a parasite? I needed that confidence back. I lifted one hand, stroking lush, dark curls back from her neck. Gazing into her eyes was like contemplating the vast potential of a new evening. They held nothing but hope and promise. The confidence I needed was right there, with her.

Finally, I understood. Like Rappaccini's daughter, Maddie had grown up tending a garden of shadows and unlife, fatally poisonous to most. She knew the consequences and risks that came with affection for my kind, maybe even better than I did. What I'd written off as parasitic, she'd watched work as symbiosis. I'd heard stories of Shi May as a kid, how he used his scrying to help people. I'd thought of him as a hero. His own daughter thought I could match his example. If I believed in her, I had to believe in myself.

I tilted Maddie's head down, kissing her lips tenderly as I recalled the focus training that kept me sane and controlled all those years. I'd need all my mental armor for this, like I'd used on her amulet. My memories from that time seeped up like groundwater in a drought, except now I understood why crafting that amulet had been such an emotionally draining task. I'd done it before, under enough duress to wipe the memory. But the only way to beat fate was to break cycles.

"Let's make some positive coincidence," I murmured against Maddie's throat.

The sensation of her flesh parting under my fangs and the sweet, hot taste of magically infused blood threatened to drown my focus. I'd left my island of carefully controlled solitude in a desperate attempt to reach civilization. I'd never make it by myself. But I wasn't alone.

"We already have that." Maddie's voice was a lifeline, her words a rope to cling to. The tide of blood washed me up on dry land. My calm returned. After I disengaged and licked her wound closed, she blinked sleepily at me, running her hand down the side of my face to stop at my chin. She kissed the corner of my mouth, then leaned against my shoulder.

I carried her to the bed and set her gently on top of the quilt. Her pulse was steady, but not as strong as earlier. I kissed the inside of her wrist before putting it down, then brushed some stray curls off her forehead. She'd need sleep, then food. I could give her that. Maddie dozed off just as I covered her with an extra blanket. I put on the Siouxsie record she'd reached for earlier, then flipped idly through the Seelie creatures book and waited.

CHAPTER SIXTEEN

Maddie

The incandescent light was almost too bright when I opened my eyes. The staccato clatter of boiling water rattled in my ears, followed by the slosh of pouring. Henry stood in the kitchen, clinking a teacup against a saucer. That sound was pure comfort. He bent at the waist as he set the tea and a plate of graham crackers on the table.

I sat up with a heaviness in my limbs like I'd slept under a lead blanket. My throat felt dry and my stomach rumbled, but nothing hurt. I shuffled toward the table. Henry pulled the chair out for me, smiling. His fangs were normal length, and his color better, even if not as sanguine as back in the cafe.

"Thanks." I sat.

"No way you're thanking me." Henry glanced at the plate and cup in front of me. "If I served you fillet mignon and lobster a thousand nights in a row, maybe I'd deserve thanks."

"Actually, this is exactly what I want right now. My stomach's still fluttery."

I inhaled graham crackers so fast the tea was still too hot when I finished. As I blew on my cup, Henry brought over another stack. I ate those too, sipping between bites. The kitchen clock read a quarter to five in the morning. Something about that bothered me.

"They're still out there?"

"Yeah." One corner of Henry's mouth tilted in a half-smile that avoided his eyes like the plague.

"Shouldn't they be gone by now?" I glanced at the clock again. "It's almost sunrise."

"Check the book." He opened it to the Spite page then pushed it across the table.

"They stay until full sunrise? That makes no sense. What kind of summoned thing does that?"

"Seelie ones, apparently. Makes perfect sense to me." Henry glanced at a spot high on one wall, practically near the ceiling. "You can't hear it yet, but the Spite's been working on getting in here for the last twenty minutes. They can chew through stone, so even though my landlord bricked up the windows, they'll get through, eventually."

"When?"

"Sometime around six, maybe earlier."

That can't happen." I flipped open my satchel, grabbed my phone. "I'm making some calls."

"Don't."

"Why not?"

"We don't know what kind of spies Brodsky might have on the rest of the group. If they're overheard, he might send something even nastier after them."

"What can be worse than a Spite?"

"More Spites."

"Okay, good point." I pulled my portable keyboard out and

propped my phone up. "I'll text instead. Can Brownies read?"

"Nope."

"Good." My fingers tapped messages to Blaine, Lynn, Josh, and Nox.

Henry dragged out a battered old Dell and fired it up. In a minute, his fingers moved with blurred speed.

"What are you doing?"

"Getting in touch with the Nocturnal Lounge crew. Fred Redford and Tony. Maybe they know how to distract it."

"I can see why you'd call Fred for that since he's a Redcap Changeling, but Tony?"

"Tony's a gossip. He works for Faeries and pays attention."

"Why not just use SMS to talk to them?"

"This is better, especially since Brodsky seems to favor using Seelie creatures."

"Nocturnal Faeries are Unseelie, huh?"

"That's a myth. When a Changeling takes a mantle, they can pick either Court. Seelies are traditional, and they like things to stay the same. Unseelies push rules to the limit. They've adapted better since the Big Reveal, so younger Changelings tithe to the King instead of the Queen. It's shifting the power balance pretty steadily. Add in centuries of bad blood and the stories each Court spreads about the other, and you've got a tempest in a teapot."

"Are the stories true?"

"Exaggerated. The only cure for that kind of misinformation is hard proof." Henry sat back and cracked his knuckles. "It's one reason Headmistress Thurston opened PPC to everyone."

"Education's the only way to fight hate." I glanced up at him. "It's why I want to teach."

Henry opened his mouth to say more but closed it when my phone beeped. The message was from Josh. Made sense. He'd be the only one remembering me. But then one came from Nox. I checked his first.

Mom's raiding Brodsky's now. I showed the message to Henry before reading Nox's.

Spites hate water. I showed that one to Henry, too.

"If they find the Grim's anchor they'll arrest Brodsky."

"Spites hating water isn't going to help us, though. I can't do Water magic. Best I can manage is hide a puddle and run through so it follows me."

"No puddles in here, especially with the faucets warded." Henry leaned back over his keyboard again. "Tony says to check that book. What's he mean?"

"No idea." I scratched my head, unsure why he'd mention that. I sent lists to Lynn and Bobby. Another message came in from Nox.

Evidence Achievement unlocked, APB out. Police tracking Brodsky now. I showed that awesome news off.

"But will they find him in time?"

"What's that noise?" I glanced at the clock again. It was half-past five now.

"That is the sound of bricks in a Spite's jaws. I've been listening to it for the last two hours now."

"But the sun's coming up. How much time do we have?"

"Maybe twenty minutes."

"Sweet Dark Night, what does Tony mean by a book?"

"Dahlia!" Henry bolted out of his seat, reaching across the table for my satchel. "She tried to stake me so you'd pick up her old book." He held up *Umbral Affinity and You*. I hadn't had a chance to look at it since the night in the basement lounge. I opened the cover, feeling a tingle as I picked up the corner of the flyleaf. Instead of flipping it, I rubbed it with my palm. An inscription showed up, all shadowy purple letters.

"Dear Dahlia," I read aloud, "someday, a dear friend will need a dark in the lightness. Make sure the right one gets this book when the time comes. Contingency and coincidence demand no less from our family. Love, Grandma Josephine. P.S. p.138." I thumbed through to the indicated page.

"Henry, look at this." I pointed at the entry.

"Sun Shield?" He blinked, his mouth wide open. He reached down and brushed the tip of his finger across the typeset-indented words. A thread of golden energy I'd never seen before surrounded the title. Gold was Luck energy, according to my textbooks. That stuff had no alignment to any magic school, element, or planetary influence. Only Tanuki could turn it. I blinked, and it vanished.

"Grandma used to tell stories about this spell. If I can figure it out, we could go for a stroll down College Hill in broad daylight." I turned my phone and keyboard toward him, then went over to the turntable. I changed the record from Siouxsie to one by The Chameleons. As I sat on the bed studying the old Umbral spell, the bass thud of *Swamp Thing*, the first song we'd danced to, filled the room. "Man the messages. I'll figure this out."

The spell needed something that absorbed sunlight, something that cast a shadow, and something sunlight would destroy. I grabbed Henry's solar-powered calculator off a stack of bills. That'd do. I'd need to attach it to something I could hold over our heads. I read that the reason I'd need something sun-vulnerable was that this spell only worked in life-or-death situations. This totally counted and meant I could use Henry as that component. I got up and pulled a big, black, bat-like bundle of metal and polyester from the umbrella stand.

"Got any super-glue?" I'd need to attach the calculator to the outside of the umbrella, then imbue the whole shebang with Umbral magic.

"Drawer under the bathroom sink." Henry didn't even glance up from typing.

The glue was right where he'd said it'd be, but so was something else. Someone, actually. A short, squat little figure with a scarred leathery face and patched conical hat rubbed their eyes sleepily. They stood, clicked its heels together, and gave me a salute. Then, they handed me the glue.

"Um, thanks." I held the tube between my thumb and forefinger. "Who're you?"

"Gee Nome, Lady." The little creature adjusted their pointy green hat and puffed out their chest. "I watch this house. Good to see a Lady with the Gentleman."

"You might want to hide a little better and then go back to sleep." I literally kicked myself for not recognizing a Gnome. Those were pure Unseelie creatures, the kind responsible for missing socks and misplaced glasses. I'd asked them a question without thinking and if I asked two more, I'd owe them a favor.

"Why should I hide, Lady?"

"A Spite's about to break in here." I peered behind Gee to see if there was anything else useful in there, while also checking for more Gnomes or whatever. "You don't want to be around when that happens."

"A Spite? Really? Who sends those anymore?" Gee rolled its eyes and tapped their foot three times on the bottom of the drawer. "I could help the Gentleman. Sun's rising, you know."

"Oh, I know. I'm Umbral, so I'm doing the Sun Shield spell." I held up the glue. "This is to put my sun absorber on my shield."

"You can't fight Spites while you do magic, Lady. And the Gentleman's weaker while the day-star shines."

"I know."

The Gnome looked up at me with a mildly expectant smirk. They knew something, maybe even had an ability that could save Henry. I'd have to ask them directly.

"What can you do to help, then?"

"Glad you asked, Lady." The Gnome smiled, displaying rows of sharp metallic teeth. I'd read somewhere that didn't have their own teeth, just whatever they could steal. This one must have gotten them from a hardware store. "I can make sure you have help. All you must do is ask for it."

"I don't imagine you'll get more specific without me asking another question." I looked into the Gnomes eyes, trying not to blink. My time was running out, but I'd know whether they'd volunteer that information in the next few seconds.

"Two items, and four of your friends to bring them."

"Fine, then." I took a deep breath. Saving Henry and my magic were important enough to owe a pure Unseelie Faerie. At least they were only a Gnome. "Will you help us?"

"Yes, Lady." The Gnome rubbed their hands together. "Make your shield, then leave this place with the Gentleman. Help will find you in time." It held its thumb and middle finger up and winked, then snapped its fingers, vanishing in a small cloud of greenish smoke.

"Who were you talking to?" Henry's voice came from the other room.

"Gnome." I closed the drawer and carried the glue out of the bathroom, shutting off the light as I went.

"Oh. Gee. Did they give you the glue?" He glanced up from the screens.

"Yeah." I waggled the plastic tube at him, then went across to the bed and opened the umbrella.

"Good." He turned my phone toward him. "Huh. Nox said she just found something that might put a dent in a Spite."

"Awesome." I coated the back of the calculator with glue. "Anything else?"

"Oh, Josh said Tony snuck away from the crime scene, talking to himself." Henry shook his head. "That guy. You never know what he's up to."

"Maybe I do, but there's no time to talk about that now." I had to focus on umbrella-imbuing and tell him about Gee. I gestured at my little project. "Once this is done, we should get out of here."

"Yeah, good point. We should keep at least a five-foot distance from the Spite if we don't want it stealing our magic." He typed something again. "Olivia says we'd better make that six feet and head west. Well, duh."

"Wow, she's up?" I had glue all over my fingers, but the calculator stuck to the fabric. Restarting the record helped me focus. "I hope they track Brodsky fast. How are you at running in the daytime?"

"Regular human speed." Henry typed one more thing, then shut down his computer. "That's one of the Spite's problems. They move at a human pace because as Sprites, their wings gave them extra oomph. Getting a head start at vampire speed will help us."

"Let me imbue this. We leave immediately after. We need as much of a head start as we can get." I put my hands on the umbrella.

The song's intro guitar riff hooked me, tightening my concentration. When the bass drum thudded out its steady beat, Henry turned up the volume. I felt the music now, in the umbrella under my hands and the bed under my crossed legs. I let all my thoughts and feelings about darkness pulse down my arms and out into the hastily crafted device.

Henry's voice mingled with Mark Burgess's as he sang along about a tune calling to him.

Shadows had been my friends for as long as I could remember, their shapes appearing on the wall between my hands and the nightlight I turned on just to create them. I summoned them all to my memory and let them power my magic. The duck and the bunny, the cat and the owl—creatures of comfort. The spider and the shark, the wolf and the dragon—creatures of predation. The church, the steeple, the tree with stubby child-finger branches—sites of safety. I gave the energy these forms and willed it into a new shape, one to protect me and the man who'd never forget me, no matter what.

My lips moved, forming words without sound around the lyrics we'd sang at the AS220 weeks earlier.

The magic enhanced mere fabric and aluminum into a shadow construct to protect us from the inevitable dawn. Shelter we could take with us, hold over our heads out in the open instead of waiting in here for that Seelie demon to tumble the wall down on us. I opened my eyes. It was done. I'd imbued my second magical item. I had to hope it'd last long enough under the sun's relentless eye.

The lyrics implored me to leave, to go now. They were right; it was time.

Henry had packed everything back in my satchel and had his own backpack over one shoulder. I took the umbrella in one hand and slung on my satchel with the other. Keeping continuous contact with the shield was a must, or I'd risk it running out of energy at the worst possible time. I stood in front of the door while Henry undid the locks.

We pounded up the stairs. I smirked at the irony of the old superstition about opening umbrellas indoors. Doing it now felt like good luck. Everything was turned on its head, by a kindly Professor who'd inexplicably turned murderer, to Seelie creatures spying and hunting us down. The street door pushed open under my hand.

The faintest hint of light tinged the horizon, its glow bloodying the sky. I went west, as Olivia advised. We'd be moving toward Brodsky's apartment, and the police were still investigating. Maybe they had emergency sun-proof blankets or light-free transport.

Henry scooped me up once we got out the door and ran as fast as he could. I heard the scrabble of broken brick and mortar behind us. Over Henry's shoulder, I saw the Spite begin their pursuit slower than I'd be at a dead sprint or even a jog. Their belly was distended, probably from eating the concrete that made up the building's foundation.

The distance between us and the creature increased as they stopped to regurgitate amalgamated stone. I wasn't sure whether

Spites could digest it eventually, but this one didn't want to try. I looked away, not wanting to watch any creature throw something up. At least we'd get a better lead while they purged.

Henry's feet carried us down Brown Street until it became Camp Street. After that, his pace slowed. I tapped his shoulder, and he put me down. Behind us, the sky was a cloudy light yellow, like a week-old bruise. The sidewalk under our feet was dark with morning dew. I linked my free arm in Henry's, and we jogged ahead. We'd lose our lead at this pace, so we'd have to stop and make a stand at some point.

When we passed Doyle Avenue, I knew there was no way we'd make it to Brodsky's building before the Spite caught up. The only park we passed had no cover at all. Everything else was closed. Even Holy Name Church was locked up like Fort Knox. Too bad. pure Faeries of any type couldn't get into churches, temples, mosques, or synagogues without an invitation from the presiding clergy.

We were on borrowed time. We'd have to buy as much more as we could. At least I knew help was coming.

CHAPTER SEVENTEEN

Henry

I put one foot in front of the other as fast as possible. The sun about to rise behind me was pure terror compared to any fire I'd seen in my unlife. It was the difference between starting at a fish jumping and having your boat capsized by a great white shark. No contest in the fear factor department.

If Maddie hadn't kept going, I might have just given up. She'd shown me more kindness, treated me more like a normal person than anyone had since the battle that claimed my humanity. Being with her felt like peace and plenty in a constant state of skirmish and scavenge. This short time with her was precious. I couldn't let the Spite take her powers. She wouldn't lose half of herself on my watch. I was ready to make a stand.

I realized she'd already been looking for a defensible place. Nothing on Camp Street would give us the advantage in a direct confrontation with a Spite. I almost wished the Grim was chasing us. At least then, Maddie's magic wouldn't be at stake.

But, of course, the fact that she'd been helping me was the reason Brodsky sent a Spite this time.

Billy Taylor Park was the only choice for a battleground. The paved basketball court gave no cover, but we'd have a clear line of sight and room to run it in circles. I nudged Maddie, indicating the park. She frowned at the open area but crossed and hopped the fence all the same.

I saw an added benefit: two buildings east of the park were tall enough to cast shadows for a few minutes. This would let me fight the Spite far enough away from Maddie to make a difference. I had to stay in the shadows or fall back to the umbrella. Vampires could drink Spite blood. I could grapple them into the regular shade and not worry about getting hungry. I'd need to bite fast so it couldn't drag me into the sun, but even if it did that, Maddie could still get away.

We ran to the west end of the paved-over park and waited. The Spite climbed the fence with some difficulty. Their back had been broken multiple times to deform it for eternity and cause them to walk on all fours. They'd been changed cruelly, robbed of intelligence and autonomy. I couldn't help but pity them. Their limpid eyes rolled, looking at us. Once they got to our side of the fence, they sighed. I got the idea the Spite didn't want to fight. I glanced at the lightening sky, sending out a prayer for them even though my old church had denied the existence of my soul.

Something white bobbed in the new light, hurtling toward us. It swam on air, but that was all I could make out with the sun behind it. I pointed. Maddie and the Spite peered at what I'd singled out in the sky.

"Olivia!" Maddie let go of my arm, waving as she called out. "Down here!"

The owl shifter folded her wings to dive. Something draped in fabric hung from her talons. She banked, dropping the item in a shadow on the other side of the basketball court. Then, she ran straight into a window, knocking herself out. She looked like a little white pile of snow on the ground by the building's back stairs. Maddie and I ran for the object she'd dropped and I pulled off the cloth. A shiny purple glass paperweight rested in my hand. I had no idea why Maddie squealed and jumped up and down.

"Give it here!" She held out her hand, and I placed the paperweight in it. She curled her fingers around the dark glass, then took a deep breath and let it out. The shield got stronger and more light-resistant as purple-black energy swirled up from the object in her hand.

The Spite paused, one foreleg in the air as hesitated. Their eyes focused on Maddie, terror as vast as mine for the sun in their gaze. I finally understood what she'd done. She'd plugged into the Grim's Anchor, tapping it like a battery. The shield would last longer, but we still had a stalemate on our hands.

I peered at the bottom of the building to check on Olivia, but she was gone. When I looked up, Josh and Nox had hopped the fence. Nox wore a pair of elbow-length dishwashing gloves. She held a shimmering sphere, her hand as far from her body as she could get it. Golden sparks whirled and pooled on its surface, sparkling in the new morning light like flying fish. Luck. Blaine's glass float.

"Stop, Spite!" Nox called to the Seelie hound as though they would listen to an Unseelie shifter. They clacked their spikes against the ground, whining eagerly like she'd brought salvation instead of demise. Beside me, Maddie gasped.

"That fishing float." She elbowed me. "It has Seelie Water magic. That's the only thing that breaks Seelie enchantments."

The Spite turned their back on us, taking slow, steady steps like a fly fisherman wading against a strong current. They got within three feet of Nox, the closest a pure Seelie could get to anything Unseelie without instinctively attacking. Nox gazed down at them, nose red and cheeks streaked with tears. She pitied the Spite, too.

Josh's jaw dropped so far he could have caught every fly on

the east side of Providence. He stared at Nox with a mixture of envy and admiration. I understood that as a young Alpha wolf, he'd wanted to save the literal and figurative day. He was about to be upstaged by a Kelpie, of all things.

Nox pursed her lips and blew a kiss at the glass float. It sailed like a soap bubble toward the Spite, drifting until it burst, spraying gold-tinged glass shards and seafoam all over the creature. They whimpered, shivers claiming their entire body. Their spikes drooped and their hunchback straightened.

That whimper became a series of screams as bone broke and reformed. Stripy scars melted, leaving smooth oatmeal-pale skin behind. A thick mane of white hair sprouted from the back of their head. Their fingers lengthened, along with arms and legs. The creature stood on two legs now, facing Nox. I watched them stretch each limb one at a time, examining them. They bowed to her, then turned toward Maddie and me y. They weren't a Spite anymore. The sea float had undone all their deformities. Well, almost all of them.

Wing bones lifted tattered strips of iridescent gossamer. This Sprite was flightless now, but at least they wouldn't live forever in pain and on their knees.

"I'm sorry for attacking. I was enslaved, but now I'm free. I owe you each a great debt, but the only thing I have to give is information." They stepped to the edge of Maddie's Umbral shield. "The Summoner is also the summoned, his will controlled by a more powerful Magus."

"Who?" Josh shook off his shock and awe, stepping forward to question the creature. Since the Sprite had agreed to pay us with information, he could do that without risk.

"I do not know, but I see that you will find out. Once enough of you turn coincidence in your favor, you will find him. Each of you four has earned three questions. The Son of Dennis has two left."

"I'll want to ask mine at some point in the future," Nox said.

"That is your right, Kelpie. But know that the Sidhe Queen will track me down at some point. Do not wait too long."

"Understood."

"I think I'll wait, too." Maddie had pocketed the Grim Anchor. "If you need to hide, find me, and I'll do what I can."

"Thank you, Shadowmistress."

"I want to use one of mine." I stepped to the edge of the shield. "The Summoner's Brownie. What's his Anchor?"

"The vampire inquires wisely." The Sprite smiled. Had I thought them so terrifying just minutes ago? "A wood cane of birch. The Summoner kept it on the floor under his bed."

"Thanks. I'll wait to ask the rest of mine if you don't mind."

"Very well." The Sprite turned back to look at Josh. "Son of Dennis?"

"I have one question no one will have the answer to yet. I want you to answer me when you've discovered it."

"Very well. Ask, and I will deliver your answer when the time comes." The Sprite gave him a pointed look. "Know that coincidence prevents me from answering a question you've already asked."

"Who will the Summoner attack after me?" Josh's jaw clenched, his eyes unblinking and intense.

I nodded. Of course. Josh had done a lot to help Maddie and me, so he had to be next on the Extramagus's list.

"Understood. I'll bring your answer when it exists and falls into the scope of my knowledge."

"I'm going to get Henry somewhere safe now." Maddie beckoned to the Sprite. "I'll hide your trail until it parts from ours."

"Thank you, Shadowmistress." It bowed at her. "I'm sorry his home isn't safe anymore."

"The basement Lounge has everything you could want." Tony leaned against the chain-link fence near where Olivia had fallen. "Go there. The Sprite can get to a bunch of hiding places from the old trolley tunnel on the way."

The Sprite froze when Tony spoke. They didn't turn around, just stood there with their back to Tony. Their facial expression was inscrutable, but their eyes held fear. When I looked again for the cat shifter, he'd gone. One white feather settled to the ground where he'd been. The Sprite finally turned their head, gazing at Maddie expectantly.

"You have to invite pure Faeries under a ward, Maddie." Nox's tone was gentle, although a little hoarse. Ha.

"Oh, right. You can come under here. You have my permission." Maddie beckoned the Sprite. They took one long step, placing themselves at my side under the Umbral sun shield. I wondered what it looked like from outside. I'd ask Josh later. There was no way I'd dare try to find out first-hand.

Our motley group made its way back to PPC on Camp Street. It had gotten late enough for the church to open. A man in a deacon's habit blinked from the steps as we walked by Holy Name. I wasn't sure whether I was the first vampire to take a shielded stroll outside during the day, but I was definitely the only one that particular deacon had seen. I smiled and waved, unsure of whether he could see me clearly or not. He rewarded me with one briefly upraised hand, then dropped into a slow-mo genuflection.

Faces peeped between blinds and curtains all along the street. Josh took point and Nox brought up the rear, making us an intimidating spectacle. One old man, bald under his black Greek fisherman's cap, stepped out the door to stand on his stoop. The slow clap of his hands as I approached accented his genuine smile. He was missing his two front teeth and seemed familiar, but I couldn't place him.

We made it to the trolley tunnel without further incident. The Sprite left so silently I couldn't imagine how anything but the Queen herself might track them. Nox went upstairs, mumbling something about helping Lynn. Josh watched her go, then shook his head like he'd been in a daze. Maybe he had. Kelpies were known for their ability to mesmerize. Once we got into the basement stairwell, Maddie dropped the shield.

"I guess this is where I say good day?" I smiled full-on, finally comfortable with that expression.

"No way." Maddie brushed past me, heading down the stairs. "Come on."

"Huh?" I followed her, even though I wasn't sure why she didn't go back to her room where she'd be comfortable.

When she opened the door to the lounge, I understood why she'd messaged Lynn and Bobby. While I'd been thinking about turning to dust, she'd been preparing for my survival. An air mattress sat in the corner farthest from the door. A mini-fridge with a Shifter Fighting League sticker on the side held a few days' worth of animal blood. There was even an electric kettle, cups and saucers, and tea. It was only bagged Bigelow Earl Grey from the dining hall, but that little touch broke me. I sat in one of the chairs and set my elbows on my knees and my head in my hands. It was all I could do to keep from crying.

"Henry, what's wrong?" I could feel the warmth of Maddie's hand through the thick leather of my jacket. I took a few deep breaths I didn't physically need before speaking.

"Nothing." I met her concerned gaze with the full force of the hope surging in my heart. "Finally, nothing. I don't feel like I'm all wrong just for being me."

"I hope you get to keep that feeling for a long time."

"As long as you're around, I think I can." I stood up, tilting my head so I wouldn't break eye contact with her. "You make me feel normal, Maddie May. I love you."

She didn't say a word, just flung her arms around my neck. Her lips met mine with no hesitation or fear.

As we headed together to my temporary bed, I realized that Maddie accepted me for who I was, knowing what that meant for me and anyone close. I used to find the night magically fascinating until I got confined to it. Since then, I'd gone through the motions and just existed. Maddie brought me back to life that morning in more ways than one.

I'd lived in a cold gray fog since I'd turned. In Maddie's arms, the color came back into everything. Drab hues brightened until I could begin appreciating the light again. Without it, darkness was stark instead of lush. I'd lost my balance, but that morning with the woman I loved, I took the first steps toward regaining it.

All it had taken was coincidence, convergence, and a little golden sliver of Luck.

CHAPTER EIGHTEEN

Maddie

We came together at the intersection of hope and despair. In the moments after, when I fell back breathing as he lay still, I remembered what Mom couldn't tell me. Convergence. I wondered whether this was it. My eyes slipped closed like a canoe slips into a creek. I drifted on sleep's current, Henry's cool hands soothing my overheated ones.

When I woke, I knew it'd be obvious that I wasn't really asleep. Still, I kept my eyes closed. The room would be pitch black, and even though I could technically see in the dark if I focused, it wasn't the same. Everything was green and gray when I did that, and I wanted to remember how Henry looked in something other than monochrome. Vampires were lucky; they saw muted colors when it got dark.

I heard the sharp click of the light switch and the soft rush of the heating electric kettle. After I rolled over and opened my eyes, I saw Henry placing teabags in the cups. I sat up, pulling my comforter around me.

"It's three in the afternoon already." He smirked. "Even Tony doesn't sleep that late."

"Well, I stayed up all night and most of the morning." I grinned, and my stomach rumbled.

"You need food." He shrugged. "No one thought I'd have a guest, I guess."

"I don't want to leave you here alone after all that." I shuddered.

"I'll be fine." He grinned.

"Hey, is that Djinn lamp still in here?" I peered at the bookshelf where I'd found it before.

"No, it's gone. I have no idea where it went." He glanced over his shoulder at the shelf, too. "We all agreed to just leave it here, right?"

"Yeah. I wonder whether one of us came back for it without telling the others, or if Brodsky came and got it after he realized we'd found it."

"What makes you think it was Brodsky's?" Henry raised an eyebrow. "It could belong to anyone."

"Aren't Djinn summoned creatures?" I sipped from my cup.

"Not exactly." Henry breathed in the scent of tea. "They're tithed Faeries, bound to serve a purpose."

"More like Fred's dad than that poor Sprite?"

"Sort of. Djinns are like magical hermit crabs—they need a home. They all got bound when the King and Queen split. It's a cool story. I wish I remembered who my Psychic mentor was. He's the one who told it to me."

"Why don't you remember him?" I couldn't imagine not being able to remember someone so important.

"I must have taken those memories out, put them away." Henry leaned his head on his hand. "The only reason I can think of is he went into hiding."

"That's sad. Maybe we'll work on finding him some time."

"Maybe. I have to go through some of my old amulets." Henry sighed. "There might be something in there. A clue. I also think it'll help with Blaine's tinfoil hat theory."

"You're waiting for Monday, huh?" Only mundane banks opened on Sundays. No one would keep amulets or magic items in one of those.

"Yeah. They have a tunnel entrance for vampires. I'll head over first thing tomorrow, see what I can find." He shrugged. "Maybe my mentor's memory is in one of the amulets. But mainly, I have to look for anything I can find on the Extramagus, Brodsky, too."

"Well, yeah." I scratched my head. "So they arrested him. But Olivia had the Grim's anchor. How'd the Police get evidence for an arrest?"

"The fang. They also found two sets of remains." Henry curled his hands around his teacup. "Horace from the Skeleton Crew made a statement last night. People forget ghosts are legal witnesses if their Mediums support them. He saw the Grim attack the Lounge."

"Is the Lounge fixed yet?" I raised an eyebrow. It had to be done by now.

"I don't know. I'll ask Tony or Fred next time I see one of them." Henry wrinkled his nose. "Ugh, I forgot. I have to give a report to Josh's dad. With Blaine."

"When?" I sat up, stretching my arms over my head. Henry stared, licking his lips. I blushed and pulled the comforter back up to cover myself. "Sorry. Didn't mean to be that distracting."

"You can distract me like that later all you want." He winked. "Supposed to be this afternoon. It's still technically afternoon, right?" Henry put on his shirt, then his jacket. "And how do I get to the tunnels from here to make it to Campus Police?"

"Why go down there? Just call."

"He said I had to do it in person."

I wrapped the comforter around myself and got out of bed, stepping over to the chair where I'd left the umbrella leaning. One touch told me it was completely depleted. I thought about recharging it, but when I picked it up the calculator clattered to the floor. I shrugged, grinning apologetically at Henry. No one would have brought super glue down here while setting things up earlier.

"How about we call him over here?" I tucked the calculator in my satchel, losing my grip on the comforter. "He could meet you in the basement."

"We could try that." Henry's eyes roamed slowly down and up my body before he looked me in the eye. "You'd need to wear something a little less revealing, though."

"Oh." I felt my cheeks heat up as I gathered my clothes. "Um, yeah."

I got dressed while Henry called Chief Dennison to explain the situation. They agreed to meet in the laundry room, which also had no windows. Henry got a bag of blood from the mini-fridge and drank that from a mug while I had some tea. After he'd finished, he poured the rest of the bag into his cup. My stomach growled again.

"You really should have some food." Henry reached out and patted my tummy.

"After you make that report." I pulled his hand up to my mouth and kissed it.

A knock came at the door. Too early for Chief Dennison. Henry went to it, asking who was there. He opened the door for Lynn.

"Nox called and told me to bring food, but you're a vampire. Isn't that the weirdest thing ever?" Lynn blinked at me, then shook her head after I activated my amulet. "Oh, okay. The food's for you then, Maddie. Here you go."

"Thanks so much." I opened the bag to see a bagel with some peanut butter and a plastic knife to spread it on. In moments I went to work setting up the super tardy meal, then tried not to eat it too fast.

"I'm going across the hall to meet Chief Dennison now. See you when it's all done, Maddie." Henry leaned down and kissed me on the mouth. Nothing super-passionate or anything, but it was enough for Lynn's eyebrow to reach new heights. Once he was out of the room, she dragged a chair next to the one I sat in and leaned forward.

"No wonder your date with Josh was so weird." She shook her head. "I mean, I thought it was strange that you were out with him instead of Henry in the first place, but still."

"What happened after I left?" I swallowed the last bite of my bagel. "With Nox and Josh and Blaine, I mean?"

"Oh, boy." Lynn shook her head. "Blaine's got a reputation and Nox was just giving him grief about it. Definitely no interest there on her part. Josh almost went ballistic, though. I've never seen him like that about a girl before. What kind of Magus is she?"

"She's not one. She's a Kelpie."

"Oh, no." Lynn sighed. "Poor Josh."

"Why?" I blinked, wondering why Lynn looked so sad. "They'd be great together. Wolves marry other shifters all the time."

"But Alphas can't marry Faerie creatures. If they get together, it'll look like the Dennisons took the Goblin King's side. The pack has to stay neutral, or it might implode."

"There's really no way?"

"Maybe. If another high-ranking pack member got together with a Seelie, then there'd be a balance. It'd have to be a sibling. I don't even know if Josh has any of those. Which rules out other options like passing on being the Alpha or going packless. If he's the only heir, he can't do either of those things."

"Well, there's a bit of hope then." I wiped my hands on the napkin from the bag.

"Dunno, Maddie. Not everyone gets a happy ending. I mean, look at Professor Brodsky."

"Him? He's got to be better off now, right?" I bit down on toasty bread and nut goodness.

"What, in jail for crimes against Extrahumanity?" Lynn gave me the Mr. Spock look while I chewed. "He'll go to trial by autumn and spend the rest of his life in prison. How's that better?"

"Better as in out from under the control of whoever had him." I ran my tongue over my front teeth, making sure they didn't have peanut butter all over them.

"Wait. I didn't hear about that." Lynn put one hand over her mouth.

"We just found that out this morning." I told her about confronting the Spite, how Nox had transformed them and the information they gave and still owed us.

"Wow. Maybe Olivia should intern with whatever legal firm is representing Brodsky. We might want a woman inside on that trial, and she's an Extrahuman Law student. Anyway, that's more info for the Blaine tinfoil hat theory pile."

"You're calling my hunt for an evil cabal of Magi a tinfoil hat theory?" Blaine leaned diagonally across the doorway, the back of his hand on his forehead. "Oh, the indignity!"

"Move it, dragon-breath." Henry shouldered past him.

"Anything for the big vampiric hero of the morning." Blaine arched an eyebrow at Lynn. "Did you hear about his stroll through the rosy-fingered streets of the dawn?"

"Maddie just told me." Lynn smiled.

"Good. Stick it in the tinfoil hat files, will you?" Blaine stuck his tongue out.

"I kind of need some actual rest, and Maddie needs more than a bagel to eat." At Henry's words, Lynn stood up.

"You sleep?" Blaine glanced at the rumpled bed. Then, he winked at me.

"Yes, actually." Henry smirked at Blaine.

"Okay, then." Blaine stepped out the door, waiting. Lynn left , brushing past him.

"I'll see you later, then." I gave Henry a kiss worthy of a Psychic impression and went off with my other friends to let him rest.

CHAPTER NINETEEN

Henry

I headed down the tunnels an hour before sunrise after confirming I could go to the Nocturnal Lounge after the bank. I waited until the teller came to unlock the tunnel entrance at seven. He opened the door, ushering me inside.

"Mr. Ricci, hello." I nodded.

"Henry Baxter. I haven't seen you since the twentieth century." The wrinkles around the little man's mouth deepened as he smiled. I grinned back, understanding that not everyone was as comfortable seeing my fangs. The gloom that thought usually caused was nowhere to be found.

"I'd like to see my box, please." I handed him my I.D. and showed him the key.

"Of course." He nodded, beckoning as he limped down the hall. I thanked Mr. Ricci when he set my box down.

Once he'd settled me in a lightproof safe deposit room, he left me alone. The box was small because my amulets were never big.

Any memory, no matter how detailed or important, would fit in an object of any size. It'd be easy to become a packrat, collecting items to put memories in. That's why everything in my box was necessary. The memories in the bank were too painful or too dangerous to keep in my head. Still, there were more than I'd have the energy or emotional fortitude to check out that day. It'd take months to get through them.

I used my key to open it and reached inside, letting coincidence guide my hand. The object I touched was smooth and almost flat, except for a concave depression on one side. Without looking, I knew this was a worry stone.

The memory came back as I pulled my hand from the box. Images of the past flooded my mind, walking down Camp Street in the morning past Holy Name Church, except it all seemed bigger. Memory me was seven years old, and I looked up at the overcast sky to the west as I walked. The sun had risen, but storm clouds kept its light at bay.

When I got to Rochambeau Street, I stopped in my tracks. One man stood over another, hunched on the ground. Bloodied fists and a pile of polished wood shards stood stark against the gray concrete. The man on the ground scrambled to pick up the pieces of a violin. He was past middle age, and when he reached out, I saw a row of numbers tattooed his arm.

"Beat it, kid." The man standing glared across the street at me. I felt a sick powerless futility, along with the understanding that no one around could stop this guy. I looked up and down Rochambeau Street, certain it'd be empty. But it wasn't.

Another kid stood on the corner diagonally from me. He was blond and tall, but my age. The kid shook his head, then extended one hand. Even across the street, I felt the chill air that knocked the attacker flat on his back. The attacker snatched a gold chain with a ring on it off the ground, then got up, and tried to run away. The survivor with the broken violin called out something about giving his mother's ring back.

A blond boy across the street dropped me a wink and extended his arm again. This time, I saw a shimmer of heat rising over his hand. He aimed his pointer finger like a gun at the thief, who screamed, dropping the ring like it was on fire. He sank to the sidewalk, clutching his blistering hand. I crossed Rochambeau, heading toward the scene as fast as I could. As I went, I did a deep breathing exercise.

"I'll keep him from bothering you ever again, Mr. Kazynski." The boy strode toward the thief, gesturing with his hand again. A stream of water shot out, and I blinked. I knew he was a Magus, but I'd never seen one who could do more than one type of magic before. "I'm way under eighteen, and my grandpa's got major connections."

"No! I'll never come back, I swear." The thief shivered in fear as the water hovered in front of his lips and nose. Mr. Kazynski looked on in abject horror. It was the expression on the victim's face that made me think the other kid's threat was genuine.

"Uh, I have a better way to stop him than that." I wasn't sure why I'd interrupted a dangerous and probably batty Magus, but it felt like the right thing to do.

"Oh, really?" His smile glittered like the grill of an oncoming truck.

"Yeah. I can make him forget he's ever seen Mr. Kazynski."

"Go for it." The kid arched an eyebrow. "Better make everyone forget while you're at it. Bad tempers and long grudges run in my family."

I nodded. As I approached the thief, the water moved out of my way. I clutched the worry stone Mom had given me and focused on everyone present. I started with the thief, touching the stone lightly to his right temple. He blinked, then headed down the hill toward North Main Street in a daze. Next, I turned to Mr. Kazynski. He'd put all the pieces of his ruined violin into its case by then. I noticed a pair of seals embossed on the velvety lining. This musician was talented enough to be honored by both Faerie Courts. I hesitated.

"What's the problem?"

"I don't want to piss off the Sidhe Queen and the Goblin King by messing with their fiddler." I pointed at the seals.

"Huh. Maybe you want to piss my family and me off even less."

"Dunno." I shrugged.

"I guess if someone has to remember it, Mr. Kazynski can." The kid smiled at the flustered violinist.

"Okay, then. You're next."

"No. You get both of us at the same time."

"What do you think I am, a master-level Psychic?"

"I think you must be to come running over here."

Again, I didn't answer him. My hand trembled a little as I held the stone up to his head. If I couldn't remove both our memories at the same time, he'd never know he'd told me not to. Then again, he seemed like the kind of kid who'd throw a fireball at my head for kicks. I went ahead and siphoned more memories into the stone, his through his forehead and mine through my hand.

The scene faded out, and I finally understood why I'd been on the wrong side of the street to catch my school bus on the first day of second grade. I felt exhausted because the stone held three perspectives. After that, I had to stop checking for the day. I thought about taking a few amulets with me, but with Brodsky in police custody, who knew what the Extramagus might throw around next. After tying the ring and worry stone together in a bandanna, I locked the box, then rang the bell to call Mr. Ricci.

I headed for the Nocturnal Lounge. Josh was in the trolley tunnel, leaning against the wall. He smelled like cloves, and cigarette butts littered the ground at his feet.

"Those things will kill you." I leaned next to him.

"Not really." He blew out a smoke ring that rivaled some of Blaine's "Wolf shifters resist the ever-living hell out of diseases."

"Huh. Who knew?" I smirked.

"Maddie did. She's up there, by the way." Josh jerked his chin at the hidden door.

"Oh?" I raised an eyebrow.

"Yeah. Tony and Fred brought her and Blaine up to look at some books." He pushed off from the wall, stretching.

"Well, what are you doing out here, then?"

"Waiting for you."

"Please don't tell me we need to have another talk." I rolled my eyes.

"Sorry." He dragged the glowing end of his nearly burned cigarette over the patchy brickwork of the tunnel wall. "We do. I swear it's not like the last one, though."

"Okay, so talk."

"It'll be a while before this happens, but my parents expect me to be the Dennison Pack Alpha someday. There's some wolf politics stuff I don't want to bore you with, but I need to run a pack before then for experience."

"What's that got to do with me?"

"We're both elbows-deep in Blaine's crazy theory. Like Nox said, we painted giant targets on our backs by helping you and Maddie, so I'm stepping up. Blaine's too out-of-touch to be in charge. Frampton and Tremain aren't leaders. It's on me to keep us focused."

"Josh, your head's going to be too big to get through the door if you don't stop pumping your ego. Get to the point already."

"See, that right there is why you're the ideal Beta." He chuckled.

"But I'm a vampire."

"I don't care. We're at PPC and handling a PPC problem. If they accept whoever's qualified, so will I." He gave me a lopsided grin. "Maddie told me she gave you a medallion. One of the old kind."

"Yeah."

"Give it here." Josh held out his hand.

The string trailed behind the bronze disk like a long tail. It rested on my upturned palm. I didn't have to wonder whether Josh could see it, either. He reached out and clasped my hand, pressing the medallion between us.

"This is a formal alliance between the vampire Henry Baxter and the Tinfoil Hat Pack. Our territory is PPC campus, India Point Park, Swan Point Cemetery, and this tunnel." Josh's voice was clear, his tone carrying unquestionable authority. "Do you accept this alliance and rank as Pack Beta?"

"Yes." I felt the unmistakable tingle of a supernatural oath. Wolf shifters had a weird type of energy, somewhere between Psychic and Magic. They say it comes from the moon. "Let's get upstairs and go to work."

"Fine." When Josh took his hand away, he left the medallion behind. I blinked, watching him slip one around his neck. The magic in the alliance pledge had split it into two pieces. I put mine on, then knocked to open the secret door.

Josh and I went up the stairs and into the Lounge proper. All the furniture was different and half the shelves new, but most everything else was the same. I thought we were alone until I saw people in my old corner of the mezzanine, heads bent over books.

Blaine looked up from his scribbled notes. He nudged Tony. Maddie sat across from Blaine, her nose in the Umbral Affinity book. Fred Redford stood off to the side, eating a foot-long steak bomb. I didn't mind. It was better for a hungry Redcap to eat food instead of the furniture. Olivia peeked out from one of the stacks, amber eyes wide as she looked at Josh's chest and then mine. Her little gasp of surprise sounded more like a sleepy hoot than anything else.

"Finally, the X Generation arrives." Blaine scribbled something else. "I'll need to know if you found anything about weird Magi at the bank, Henry."

"Hi, Olivia." Josh ignored Blaine and nodded at her.

"Hoo, boy, you've gone and done it this time."

"What?" Blaine looked up at Josh and me, then paled. "Oh, no, you didn't."

"What's the big deal?" Fred rolled his eyes. "It's only a couple of bromance necklaces."

"No, it's not, but you wouldn't know." Blaine shook his head. "You can't see that magic."

Tony stared at the medallion halves like he could see something. I remembered back to the first Grim attack, how he'd made a Glamour. I almost asked what he saw, but I remembered my promise. One of these days, someone would figure out what his deal was.

"Magic's probably mine, from when I worked on it in lab. Wait, did you say necklaces? Plural?" Maddie looked at the medallion halves. "What kind of magic is that? It's definitely not Umbral."

"It's an alliance medallion. I used it for its intended purpose." Josh put his hands on his hips. "Things will get crazier around here the more we find out, so I formalized things."

"I ain't a pack animal." Tony practically bristled.

"You don't have to be." Josh's tone was full of bravado. He knew as well as I did that we'd need Tony's help.

"So, you want to know what I saw at the bank, Blaine?" I had to change the subject before we ended up with a cat and dog fight on our hands.

"Yeah. But first, look here." He flipped open an old magazine. Old as in published when I was still in diapers. "Check this guy out. He might be our mysterious magus."

The article was from a 1972 Magiczine, a publication that looked like gibberish to anyone but Extrahumans. The man in the picture was blond, tall, and haughtily imposing in a way that put both Josh and Blaine to shame. He looked familiar. If I'd seen the article the night before, I'd have thought him some random Alphahole.

"Richard Stanhope, Extramagus." I read the caption aloud. "He looks a lot like someone I saw in a stored memory I found this morning." I described what I'd seen to the group. Olivia watched without blinking the entire time, the pen in her hand moving back and forth across a moleskin journal. She held it up for everyone to see the drawing she'd made.

"Wow. This could be that kid's grandpa."

"Yeah. Too bad I have no idea who that kid is." I sighed. "I bet he's the Extramagus causing all this trouble."

"Well, why not this Stanhope guy? It says here that he doesn't like Magi and Psychics mingling with us rabble." Tony pointed at one of the article's quotes.

"Because he died right at the start of the Big Reveal." I stepped over to the bookshelf behind Maddie. "It's in here. He died hiding magic artifacts when it looked like Extrahumans would be outed. Says House Harcourt had something to do with it, too, Blaine."

"What?" Smoke came out of Blaine's mouth with the word. He took a few deep breaths before speaking again. "Mom and I are having a talk later." He looked back down at the table. "Um, whenever she feels like it."

"Anyway, at least we can try to look up all his relatives." Maddie tapped her phone, entering the name in her Evernote app. "I have a subscription to Ancestry dot com. I'll check it once I'm at an actual computer. In the meantime, do we have any idea what Brodsky's telling the police?"

"He can't remember anything." Josh rolled his eyes.

"Makes sense if our Extramagus was controlling him." Blaine tapped his pencil against the magazine. "Any idea how?"

"We saw a bunch of sleep-aids in his apartment." Josh ran his hand over his head, spiking up his hair. "Maybe that's got something to do with it."

"But sleep help is a Psychic thing, not magic." Olivia peered out from behind the bookcase again.

"Amulets can be Psychic and Magic at the same time." Maddie glanced up. "Mine sure is."

"So you're saying you think the Extramagus took a sleep amulet and put Mind magic in it?" Blaine blinked.

"Why not?" Josh shrugged.

"Hmm, I don't know. More mysteries." Blaine stroked his chin. "You think I could get a look at it sometime?"

"That's the problem. There wasn't anything like a psychic sleep aid at Brodsky's apartment." Josh shook his head. "Not even in the secret compartment the Sprite told us about. They found the second fang in there, though."

"Maybe you didn't look hard enough." Fred's voice came out muffled around the last of his sandwich. "He was a Summoner with Faerie minions. A Brownie, a Spite, and a Pixie, right? So the amulet might be under a Glamour or in a Faerie Circle or a Gnome's junk pile."

"Could you check that?" Josh scratched his chin.

"I could, but it'd be stupid to bother." Fred swallowed. "If your Extramagus was careful enough to work through that poor Brodsky guy, he would have gotten that amulet back by now."

"Good point. Mind magic's super regulated." I sighed, glad I knew all the illegal things for once. "The police would trace that fast."

"Leaves us at a temporarily dead end." Blaine flipped the magazine closed.

"So, what now?" Maddie shook her head. "We've still got a problem. He'll come after Henry and me again, right?"

"Um, no. Because both of you were direct targets of the Extramagus, just like Lynn and Bobby were last semester." Blaine sighed. "It's someone else's problem now."

"So one of us is next?" Olivia glanced up from stowing the journal and pen in her bag.

"Awesome." Josh cracked his knuckles. "Let him bring it. He'll have to go through me first."

"Not you. Nox." Maddie tucked her phone away. "She's the one who neutralized the Spite. It would have gotten Henry if it hadn't been for her."

Josh looked like a sail on a day with no wind. I punched his shoulder. His jaw tightened.

"Hey, you have help. Isn't that what a pack's for?"

"Exactly." Blaine smiled, then chuckled over Tony's second attempt to insist he wasn't no pack animal for nobody nohow.

CHAPTER TWENTY

Maddie

The sky looked like lapis lazuli to the east and boulder opal to the west when I met Henry at the tunnel next to Water Place Park. I took his hand, and we walked along the mosaic wall toward the park proper. I ran my hand along one and found a paw-print made by a shifter artist when this wall went up.

Even though Providence is on the coast, I smelled no salt in the air. Henry probably did, though. The park's eponymous water came from the Woonasquatucket River. Our footsteps mingled, echoing across the round man-made pond on the cobblestones along the RiverWalk. The braziers were empty, unlit at this time of year. WaterFire didn't start until mid-March. I looked forward to seeing it with someone who'd remember me this year.

I stopped walking when we got to a bench. Henry sat down, pulling me close to him and looking into my eyes. I smiled. I'd left the bronze amulet at home, saving the rest of its power for the remainder of my class. Everyone we were meeting would remember me.

"I'm not ready to go over there just yet."

"Agreed." He pulled me closer, sweeping a stray curl off my left cheek. His kiss took my breath away. It was a few moments before I found my voice again.

"Why me?" I stroked the back of his neck.

"I'd forgotten how to feel until you came along." He smiled. "My life was like Kansas at the beginning of *The Wizard of Oz*. That happens to vampires sometimes, but you already knew that."

"Yeah, I do. If Mom and Dad hadn't been destined before he got turned…" I couldn't finish that thought. I couldn't even imagine how to.

"You said something about a contingency the other night. Something about your mom mentioning it." Henry was a Psychic. He knew what that meant to a Precog.

"Yeah, well, she says that's why they're visiting." I leaned my head on his shoulder and sighed, looking out at the untroubled water.

"They really didn't tell you they were in town until after they got here?" Henry put his arm around me.

"That's life with a Precognitive mother. I'm used to her knowing where I'll be before I do." I looked up at him.

"Harsh during the teenage years, huh?" He rubbed my arm.

"Yeah, no actual sneaking out of the house or anything since she was immune to my Umbral Affinity." I ran my hand through the short hair at the back of his neck. "Anyway, are you nervous?"

"You'd better believe it. At least I don't have to worry that they hate vampires or Psychics. But it's unsettling how they have something they need to tell me. Should I be worried?"

"I'd say no, but…" I shrugged. "Who knows?"

"Then let's find out already." Henry stood up and took my hand. He led me around the rest of the RiverWalk, back toward

Luxe Burger. He waited until we could see the door. "You ready?"

"Okay." I took the lead. We headed into the restaurant together like we had just four nights before. At least, this time, Henry wasn't starving.

I saw Mom and Dad seated, and they waved us over. Just a handful of years ago, I might have been embarrassed, but now I understood. They seemed corny in their enthusiasm because they'd been through some strange times together. They appreciated what they had so much, they didn't care what people thought when they acted happy about it. Folks like them made people like the Extramagus even more mysterious. Why reduce happiness when it was so hard to come by in the first place? Why not foster it, let it grow and spread instead?

Dad kept his mouth in a straight horizontal line but winked at Henry, anyway. Mom pulled me close, whispering about how cute a couple we made. She asked too loudly whether I'd been eating enough. He laughed and said he could tell it must be the perfect amount. Mom didn't order anything. Dad sipped a Bloody Mary.

"You're wondering what we had to tell you that was so important we couldn't do it over the phone." Dad stirred his drink with the stick of celery that even living people never ate.

"It was the contingency, of course." Mom leaned her cheek on her hand. "I saw that you'd find someone and he'd do something momentous. And it happened, so we're here to tell you that it's time for us to use that license."

"Wait, what?" Henry's brow crinkled in confusion. "I don't understand. I didn't do anything. It was our friend Nox, the Kelpie. She freed a Spite."

"Oh, Maddie told me about that already. You did something more important than just win a battle." Mom fluttered her hand. "You took a step toward stopping a war."

"It's that." Dad nodded at the middle of Henry's chest. "Your alliance with the wolf shifter."

"But I didn't tell you about that." It was my turn to make my face do a confusion gymnastics routine.

"You didn't have to." Mom tapped her temple. "I saw the whole thing before it happened, of course."

"And I saw it once it did." Dad smiled. "It's been decades. Well, you know exactly how long ago the last vampire-wolf pack alliance dissolved. You've got a bit of a reputation, Henry Baxter. Everything I've heard is good."

"That's a huge compliment coming from Shi May. Thank you." Henry blinked, smiling back. I squeezed his hand under the table.

"All the same, I'm still Maddie's father. I'm also a vampire, like you. I know what it's like to love a mortal woman and have to wait. You'll take your time with her. Let her have her education uninterrupted. Make sure everything is done within the law."

"I will, sir. I know how the laws for turning work, and still remember what it was like to be a fledgling."

"Good, then we won't have a problem." Dad took the celery out of his drink and laid it on a napkin.

"Dad, seriously?" I rolled my eyes. Henry froze, looking more than a little frightened. "Okay, obligatory embarrassed-daughter act all done. For now."

"She gets that from me, you know." Mom's conspiratorial wink started everyone at the table laughing.

I spent way more of my time laughing after that. Knowing for sure that I had people in my life who remembered me made all the difference. When the rest of my friends came through the door in a raucous group, it only took a few moments for them to notice I was there. Lynn and Bobby blinked and scratched their heads, taking the longest to remember me. Olivia glanced at a journal and smiled, then took the first chair she got to at the table across from ours. Nox sat next to her, leaning back in her seat and making herself at home.

Tony shrugged out of his trench coat, draping it over his chair before sitting down. He made a snide remark to Bobby about cheeseburgers and Internet memes, then dropped me a wink. One corner of Josh's mouth tilted up as he mock-saluted Henry. He turned his chair around and sat backward on it across from Nox.

"So, what do you call this ersatz pack of ours anyway?" Blaine took his seat almost primly by comparison as though trying to prove that some shifters had decent table manners.

"You're going to love it." Josh lowered his voice when he spoke, so I didn't hear what he said, even though I knew the answer already. His reply had Lynn giggling and Bobby slapping his knee. Olivia cocked her head to one side and blinked, and Tony smirked. Nox whickered a laugh.

"Really? Tinfoil Hat?" Blaine blew a tiny wisp of smoke out his nose. "Can't you take anything seriously?"

"No reason to. Everything else is serious enough. Gotta grab a little light while we can." The waitress interrupted him, coming over to take their orders.

He was right. A little light made a big difference. Without it, what was darkness anyway? I leaned against Henry and looked at my parents again, certain I had all I'd need, even if we lived for centuries.

SAY WATKINS?

**A Providence Paranormal College
Short Story**

"Now get out of my lecture hall and hit some books before your grades hit Ground Zero."

I watched the second-semester sophomores shamble out like a zombie horde. Spring semester always began with a sort of mass somnolence. I yawned.

"It better not be contagious."

"It's not."

"Who said that?"

"Ahem."

I peered up into the nosebleed seats, but no students lurked. After turning to check behind the whiteboard, I almost tripped right over something. Leaning over for another look, I saw that the impossible had happened. I was wrong.

"Gnomes. Just what I need." I rolled my eyes and lifted my foot to step over the little Faerie.

"That's absolutely right. Well, almost." The Gnome winked.

"I'm not asking you what you mean by that." I kept my foot in the air, looking around on the ground for more Gnomes.

"Really?" The Gnome chuckled. "Then get off my lawn, whippersnapper!"

"That's usually my line." I put my foot down safely on the other side of my annoying little visitor.

"I know. I'm a fan."

"No, you're a Gnome." I rolled my eyes.

"You're not funny, you know."

"I don't care. I'm not here to be funny. I'm here to teach too much material to too many students. Usually, they're the ones who can't get things under control." My shoulders sagged. "But now I'm in their shoes, thanks to old Brodsky being sloppy and getting himself arrested."

"Right. It's why I'm here." The Gnome gave a snappy little salute. "To help."

"Gnomes don't help projection Psychics for no reason." I tucked my folder of lecture notes into my satchel.

"I have a reason." The Gnome's eyes cut away to the right.

"Lay it on me, then." I jiggled the giant steel-coated Bubba travel mug that I kept my high-octane coffee in, found it still half-full , and took a sip.

"No."

"Huh." I scratched my head. No self-respecting pure Faerie did mortals favors unless it was payback. And I didn't have any IOUs from Gnomes. But someone I knew did, once upon a time. And hadn't a Gnome been involved in the debacle over inter-session with said person's old apprentice? "Edgar, that memory-bending bastard."

"Not a nice thing to call your brother." The Gnome grinned, showing a mouth full of steel bits and bobs.

Gnomes had no natural teeth. Instead, they made them from items related to whoever's debt they'd dealt with recently. My missing brother had used metal for most of his memory trinkets in his practicing Psychic days. This little Unseelie Faerie must owe Edgar something. I wondered whether it was from way back or more recently. Could the Gnome have information I wanted?

The simplest explanation always makes the most sense, even in Extrahuman affairs.

"In any case, there's no point in using me to satisfy your debt. I haven't seen Edgar for decades. He never calls, he never writes, he's not been seen since floral prints and flannels were all the rage." I glanced at my watch, in a near-panic because I was exactly one minute late to Brodsky's next Extrahuman History section. "Good day."

"But you need help."

"I said, good day!" I stamped with one foot perilously close to the Gnome. Not a flinch from the Faerie's direction.

"Gnomes are Unseelie, so there's nothing good about a day for my kind." Tiny fists socked themselves against mini hips. "And I'm helping you whether you like it or not."

I opened my mouth to say something else, I don't even know what. Everything around me streaked and flashed, like when The Enterprise goes Warp except in reverse. I blinked and held my hands out in case I was falling. But no such thing had happened. Everything went back to normal seconds later. Almost.

Light from the ceiling flashed back from the face on my watch and into my left eye. But my right eye saw and my brain comprehended immediately.

"You moved us five minutes backward."

"Ayup." The Gnome winked, then clapped their tiny hands together. "Now get it under control and move your backside, so you're not late."

"That's my line!" I pulled my fingers apart to keep from making fists. After that, I filled them with the satchel and bucket of coffee. Slinging the satchel over one shoulder freed up one of my hands, essential if I expected to open the door once I'd scaled Mount Classroom.

Marching up the aisle of the lecture hall, I passed row after row of empty seats. The sophomores might have been figuratively zombified, but at least they picked up after themselves. Then, way up in the back, I found something.

"Phillips!" I couldn't clap to wake the sleeping Kelpie, so instead I balled up a fist and clanged it against the stainless steel jug/mug hybrid in my other hand. Under my breath, I mumbled, " Why do I always have to get the sleepy ones?"

"Say wha—" A long snort and a short jolt interrupted her words. "Watkins! I mean, what? I mean, Professor, sir." She sat up, flinging dank hair out of her face in a completely futile effort to make herself presentable.

Nox failed miserably at that, of course. She'd drooled over half her chin, and her coat had left an impression like a line of stitches on her cheek. Her eyes were so bloodshot I could barely discern her iris color, and she had a puffiness about her visage that hadn't been there during Fall semester. The Kelpie was not okay.

"Listen, you don't have to go home, but you can't stay here, Phillips." I tapped my wingtip-clad toe in her general direction. "I've got students waiting for me across the hall, so scram."

"Oh." Nox pulled the lapels of her coat closer together, then hoisted an unusually large rucksack up to her right shoulder. "Uh, okay." She blinked, and her lower lip trembled.

I didn't have time for this. But Miss Phillips looked like she'd been sleeping in lecture halls instead of wherever she was supposed to. Even worse, she looked like she was about to cry over it. I'm harsh and stodgy and like it that way, but I'm not heartless. Kids at the College should never be left without options. As far as I'm concerned, the only person who had any right to limit a student's choices was said individual.

"Listen, you're Unseelie. The Nocturnal Lounge is technically open twenty-four seven. Nobody bothers going there in the daytime except the ghosts on the skeleton crew and their hippie Medium, though." I pushed the door to the lecture hall open with one hand. "Now skedaddle already."

"Um." The lanky kid somehow managed to duck under my outstretched arm. "'Kay. Thanks." Phillips scuttled along the corridor, reminding me for all the world of one of those water-walking bugs.

Crossing the corridor, I made a mental note to have a chat with Jeannie La Montaigne, the Resident Assistant. She'd be able to figure out Nox Phillips' damage way better than a crusty old professor like me.

When I put my hand on the latch to open the door, I yawned again. Glancing down at my watch, I wondered how four of the five gnome-stolen minutes had gone by already. Was my brain old enough to perceptually warp time? What had I just been thinking of doing? Could it be Alzheimer's, like poor Mr. Meyer?

"Ahem." The Gnome peered up at me, showing off their steel smile. I realized that the makeshift teeth looked a bit crooked, which meant it was about time the Faerie replaced them. I wondered what, or potentially who, the Gnome's empty gums waited for.

"Er—" I wanted to ask. One more question would be safe. But there wasn't time. I walked inside the other lecture hall and strode down to the front, fully prepared to begin class but grouchier than usual about it.

That entire year was turning out to be one of my worst in so many ways. Temporal obligations were only the beginning of my troubles.

The series continues with *Of Wolf and Peace coming April 29, 2021.*